TIME OF THE RABIES

The Basque Series

BOOKS BY ROBERT LAXALT

The Violent Land: Tales the Old Timers Tell

Sweet Promised Land

A Man in the Wheatfield

Nevada

In a Hundred Graves: A Basque Portrait

Nevada: A Bicentennial History

A Cup of Tea in Pamplona

The Basque Hotel

A Time We Knew: Images of Yesterday in
the Basque Homeland

Child of the Holy Ghost

A Lean Year and Other Stories

The Governor's Mansion

Dust Devils

A Private War: An American Code Officer in
the Belgian Congo

The Land of My Fathers: A Son's Return to
the Basque Country

Time of the Rabies

UNIVERSITY OF NEVADA PRESS ▲▲ RENO & LAS VEGAS

TIME OF THE RABIES

Robert Laxalt

The Basque Series
Series Editor: William A. Douglass

University of Nevada Press, Reno,
Nevada 89557 USA
Copyright © 2000 by Robert Laxalt
All rights reserved
Manufactured in the United States
Design by Carrie Nelson House

Library of Congress Cataloging-in-
Publication Data
Laxalt, Robert, 1923–
Time of the rabies / Robert Laxalt.
    p.   cm.
— (The Basque series)
ISBN 0-87417-350-7 (alk. paper)
1. Basque Americans—Fiction.
2. Sheep ranchers—Fiction.   3. Ranch
life—Fiction.   4. Rabies—Fiction.
5. Nevada—Fiction.   I. Title.
II. Series.
PS3562.A9525 T56 2000
813'.54—dc21   00-008546

First Printing
09 08 07 06 05 04 03 02 01 00
5 4 3 2 1

For my uncle Pete

In the 1920s, an episode of rabies swept through the sheep bands of western Nevada. This book is based in part on that epidemic.

TIME OF THE RABIES

At the base of the jumble of boulders, there was a black hole that penetrated the hillside. The dozing coyote's attention was caught by a flutter of movement as the bat emerged from the hole.

If the coyote were equipped to wonder about such things, he would have been surprised to see a bat come out into the daylight. Night was the time for bats to emerge from their subterranean chambers.

The coyote watched as the bat fluttered erratically over the tops of the sagebrush that concealed the hole in the boulders. The bat seemed to have no destination at all, until it saw the coyote. Then its flight straightened as it clasped its webbed wings together and dived at the coyote.

Never having been confronted by such an attack, the coyote raised his head in wonder. The next thing he knew, the bat had fastened itself on his nose, sinking its eyeteeth into the tender flesh.

The coyote yelped in his surprise, which turned quickly into anger. His paw reached out to strike the bat away from his nose. To his amazement, this was not an easy task. The bat's hold was like a vise. The coyote raised his other paw, grasped the bat, and pulled. Finally, he succeeded in tearing the bat loose, but not until he had caught a glimpse of the bat's vampirelike teeth stained with blood.

In a rage, the coyote closed his jaws shut on the bat and crushed it into a tangle of bones and webbing. With a toss of his head, he threw the bat into the sagebrush. Then he tended to his hurt. The tip of his tongue barely reached the bloody punctures the bat had made in his nose. The coyote licked at the wound and was reminded of the time a spitting bobcat had clawed his nose when he had tried to get at her cubs in their den.

This wound, however, had a different quality about it. The coyote's nose felt as hot as fire. There was a spring nearby, and the coyote trotted to it and dipped his nose into the icy water until relief came.

Then the coyote went back to his rocky ledge and resumed his patient watch on the flock of sheep grazing across the ravine.

The coyote was not to be granted surcease from his troubles. This time, the big tawny sheepdog that was guarding the band of ewes sighted his movements. Barking in outrage, the sheepdog rushed like a whirlwind at his old enemy, leaping over the tops of the sagebrush in his pursuit.

Disgusted at the way his day had turned out, the coyote took to his heels. He was lean and fast and easily outdistanced the sheepdog. When the dog gave up the chase and went back to his sheep, the coyote rested until his breath had come back and then turned his attention to hunting out a jackrabbit. He stopped first, however, to paw at the burning puncture wounds the bat had inflicted on his nose.

* * *

The coyote roused from his sleep when the moon was high in the sky. He awoke out of sorts with the world, so much so that he growled at his mate when she awakened.

His mate approached him subserviently, hoping to better his mood. Instead, the coyote rushed snarling at her. She leaped away from his attack, but not before the coyote had bitten her on the shoulder. When that happened, the bitch gave up trying to assuage her mate. She simply fled away.

To her surprise, the coyote did not pursue her. Instead, he sat back on his haunches and howled. It was not a hunting or a courting call. It was the howl of an animal in pain.

A day passed. When night came again, the coyote was wandering aimlessly through the sagebrush hills. He needed sleep desperately, but sleep had been denied him through the day. All that his body would allow him to do was run. He roamed through the sagebrush until he came to a stream. Beside sleep, he needed water. His thirst was raging. He plunged his muzzle into the water and tried to lap and suck liquid down his throat. He succeeded in wetting his mouth, but his throat constricted when he tried to swallow. The liquid simply dribbled out of the corners of his mouth.

When drinking failed him, he was suddenly obsessed with the desire to bite. Not bushes or wood, but living flesh. He flushed a rabbit out of hiding, but he was too weak to pursue it. The coyote could not know it, but he had slowly been losing his senses.

By the time dusk was falling and he smelled the band of sheep, he was mad.

CHAPTER 2

Nazario the Basque sheepherder had the distinct impression that something was following his band of sheep when they topped the ridge.

The impression grew stronger as the band trailed through the sagebrush toward the lambing corrals at the bottom of the slope. The band was tired after a long day's grazing in the desert hills. The ewes, heavy with lambs, moved noddingly forward, trailed by the big, tawny sheepdog, Campolo. But Campolo was nervous, too, and kept making little forays into the sagebrush.

Nazario stopped to survey the land around him, but the falling dusk made it difficult to see anything out of the ordinary. When the short hairs on the back of his neck began to rise, Nazario knew for certain that something was out there in the sagebrush. He eased his scarred carbine off his shoulder and levered a cartridge into the breech.

At the bottom of the slope, sheep corrals and pens began to

take shape in the dusk. The sheep quickened their pace toward the wide gate that was opened for them by Michel, a young herder fresh from the Basque Country of France. Hay and water would be waiting for them in the big corral.

Campolo suddenly burst out into a frenzy of barking, and Nazario saw their pursuer for the first time. It was a coyote, a big one, but gaunt, as if he were starving.

Nazario raised his carbine to take aim, then lowered it quickly. The coyote was moving uncertainly toward him, unexplainedly stumbling into a rock boulder in the sagebrush. Nazario knew then that something was radically wrong.

The coyote's collision with the boulder seemed to change his direction. He veered in a straight line toward the last of the band trotting through the open gate, making it impossible for Nazario to shoot without hitting a ewe. He slung the carbine back to his shoulder, picked up his walking staff, and started running toward the sheep entering the big corral.

At the gate, Michel had seen the coyote, too. Picking up a long sheephook leaning against the corral, he was making his way through the sheep in an effort to intercept the coyote. At Nazario's shouted warning, Michel stopped in his tracks.

The coyote for sure was actually going to attack the sheep. He was staggering as if he were drunk, but he was moving in a straight line toward the last of the ewes going through the gate. "Campolo!" Nazario shouted to his dog. "Stop him!"

Campolo rushed forward and then stopped before he reached the coyote. It was as if he were reluctant to close with the animal, which was unlike a seasoned coyote fighter like Campolo. He was barking furiously, but he was staying out of reach of the coyote.

The coyote had chosen his target, a woolly ewe heavy with obvious twin lambs, wobbling as she tried to keep up with the band. It was then that Michel's little border collie burst upon the scene and flung himself at the coyote's throat. The coyote snapped sideways, slashing the dog's muzzle, and then closed in on his target. Foregoing the ewe's woolly neck, he clamped his jaws shut on her mouth. The ewe shook her head ponderously, but she could not dislodge the coyote's grip.

Nazario and Michel arrived at the same time at the scene of the struggle. Nazario poked the muzzle of his carbine into the coyote's ear, but he did not dare to pull the trigger. The bullet would have gone through the coyote's head all right, but the velocity would carry it into the ewe's body.

Michel was beating at the coyote with the metal head of the sheephook, but this accomplished nothing. The coyote was still snarling. Nazario and the young herder exchanged one baffled meeting of the eyes, and then Nazario dropped his carbine, took hold of the coyote's tail, and pulled with all his might. But even that could not dislodge the animal.

In desperation, Nazario picked up a rock. Holding the coyote by the scruff of his neck, he pounded the animal's head into a pulp. The tactic was successful. Coyote and ewe were parted. The ewe, weak and bleeding from her torn mouth, managed to get to her feet and stumble into the corral.

"*Debria!*" Nazario cried out breathlessly in Basque. "He's a devil! What in the hell is going on?"

Michel had shut the gate and was examining the border collie's white muzzle, bloody from the coyote's slashing swipe at him.

"Get the boss!" Nazario ordered Michel. "He's got to see this." The young man vaulted the fence and crossed the corral in the direction of the ranch house.

In the thickening dusk, they huddled around the body of the coyote. A kerosene lantern cast its uncertain glow over men and dogs and the coyote.

Two more herders had come from the bunkhouse, and Pete Lorda, whose ranch it was, had come from the ranch house. He was leaning over the coyote's smashed head as Nazario related the bizarre account of the coyote's attack. "He wouldn't let go. He had a grip like iron on that ewe's mouth. Look! His jaws are still clamped shut."

Lorda reached one hand out to turn the animal over so that he could see better, then pulled it back quickly. "See that slobber around the damned thing's mouth?" he said, shaking his head. "Don't touch him unless you got your gloves on. He's sick with something."

"Or just plain loco," said Nazario.

"Throw him in a shed and lock the door," Lorda said to the two herders who had joined them. "I don't want the dogs messing around with him until we find out what's the matter."

He seemed to hear the whimpering of Michel's border collie for the first time. He turned, and Michel held out the little collie so that Lorda could see for himself the gash the coyote had inflicted.

"Get some sheep-dip on that cut before it gets infected," Lorda said. In afterthought, he added to Nazario, "Find the ewe and pen her for tonight. We'll treat her in the daylight. Her mouth must be a mess."

"It is," said Nazario. Picking up the sheephook, he let himself into the corral where the sheep had gone.

"Whatever is going on here, I don't like it," said Lorda.

Tristant, a grizzled old sheepherder who had come from the bunkhouse, cleared his throat and started to say something. The clang of the dinner triangle rode over his words, and Lorda said, "Save it for dinnertime." He straightened his tall, spare frame. "We better get to the table. That dinner bell sounds like Mama's mad already." He started toward the ranch house in long strides. "Don't forget to wash up good," he called back. "You know how she is about clean hands and faces."

"We know," one of the herders laughed.

CHAPTER 3

Mama Lorda was there to greet them as they trooped through the back door into the kitchen. She was a full-breasted woman with barely graying braids caught up in back in a neat bun. She looked and was a no-nonsense Basque matriarch, a woman to be reckoned with.

The ranch workers held out their hands like children for her inspection. They had dutifully scrubbed them clean at the pump outside the bunkhouse. That they had passed muster was acknowledged by a curt nod of her head. Then they were free to find their places on the benches along the sides of the long oilcloth-covered table at the end of the kitchen.

The warmth exuding from Mama Lorda's immense cook-stove was welcome in this frosted time between winter and spring. The Sierra to the west of the winter desert range and the ranch was still white with snow, and when the wind blew, it was cold even in the desert. In the Sierra lay the summer range that surrounded the high mountain lake called Tahoe.

In June, after the shearing of the sheep by itinerant Mexican crews from southern California, Pete Lorda's bands would fatten on the luxuriant grasses that had been growing under the mountain snowpacks.

The table was set and waiting for the men. A solitary light bulb fed by the single power line from Carson City illuminated the table. Places were set with sturdy plates that could bear long wear. In the middle of the table, a huge oval loaf of sourdough bread rested with a knife impaled in its center. By custom, each man cut his own thick chunk of bread. Bottles filled with red claret wine lined the table, also by custom, and tin cups waited in front of each plate. Still-steaming tureens of soup waited at each end of the table.

Except for copper-skinned Grant, the Indian handyman who chopped the firewood and doubled as blacksmith and tracker for missing bunches of sheep, the faces of the herders and of the cowboys, Slim and Tex, were red and cold-burned.

Tall and spare with graying hair and moustache, Pete Lorda, the boss, sat at the head of the table and was the first to be served. As soon as he had filled his soup bowl, the others were free to serve themselves. The dinner began with vegetable soup that had been simmering since morning. When that was done with, the main courses would be served by the Lordas' only child, Marie, just out of high school and in her late teens.

There was little conversation as the dinner progressed with servings of lamb stew, canned tomatoes, french-fried potatoes, and beefsteaks from Lorda's steers. The first priority before talk was the satisfying of appetites made ravenous from hard work and cold.

When Pete Lorda had pushed his plate away and was nibbling at cheese for dessert, he nodded to the old herder, Tristant.

"You started to say something out there about that loco coyote," he said.

Tristant emptied his wine cup. "I don't know," he said reluctantly. "I don't want to cause worry by saying something foolish. I could be dead wrong."

"Give us a chance to judge that," said Lorda.

"All right," said Tristant. "I was herding sheep in New Mexico ten years back."

"Go on," said Lorda.

"They got a big cave full of bats down there," said Tristant. "Carlsbad Cavern or something like that. The bats come out at night but not in the daytime. One day, one of them bats came out in the daytime and fastened onto a sheepdog. The herder had to jerk that bat's teeth off his dog, he was holding on so hard." He turned to Nazario. "Just like the coyote you had to pull loose from the ewe."

"I know what you're going to say," said Tex the cowboy. "I was in New Mexico same time as Tristant, cowboying."

"So?" said Lorda, impatiently.

"Bats carry the rabies."

Lorda was sobered by the word *rabies*.

"What happened?"

"All hell broke loose," said Tristant. "That dog bit another dog, and then he fought a coyote. Both the dog and coyote started biting everything within sight."

"Even the horses," said Tex.

"How did they stop it?" asked Lorda.

"I don't know," said Tristant. "A Mexican herder got bit and died. When I heard that, I quit and came to Nevada." He paused uncertainly. "I heard later that the rancher had to shoot his best sheepdogs."

"So did others," said Tex. "As for me, I made tracks north as fast as I could."

"You mean to tell me a man can die from this rabies?" asked Lorda.

"The Mexican sure as hell did," said Tristant.

Lorda was thoughtful. "New Mexico is a hell of a long way from here in Nevada." He got up from the table. "Just for safekeeping, I'm going to call the doctor. Get him out here tomorrow."

"He's not a doctor," corrected his daughter, Marie. "The right word is *veterinarian*."

"Same difference," smiled Lorda. "You're so smart."

CHAPTER 4

Nazario had brought his band of sheep back to the lambing corrals just in time. The ewes began dropping their lambs at daybreak, and the drop had been continuing at a steady pace since then.

The big corral was filled with activity as Nazario, Tristant, and Michel lifted each newborn lamb with the crook at the end of their sheephooks and carried them gently to the sides of the corral fence. The lambs mewed while their mothers licked them clean and then nudged them toward a teat for their first taste of milk. Once that had been accomplished, the lambs gathered strength with each gulp of milk. Within an hour of feeding and gathering warmth from the spring sun, they were able to begin the complicated process of learning to walk.

Sometimes a lamb died during birth, and at other times, a mother would refuse to accept her lamb. Then the herders would skin a dead lamb, make a jacket out of its hide, and slip it on a motherless lamb. The orphan and a lambless ewe were then confined together in a pen until the lamb had suckled for the first time, so to be accepted by the mother who had lost her lamb in birthing.

In the shed at the end of the line of pens, a council of war was going on between the veterinarian, Doctor Cady, and Pete Lorda. With gloved hands resting on his knees and wire-rimmed glasses perched on his nose, the veterinarian was peering closely at the long, gaunt body of the dead coyote.

Doctor Cady had made Nazario take him step-by-step through the incident from the first moment Nazario had sighted the coyote in the dusk.

Nazario did so, recounting the coyote's veering off-course from his collision with the boulder to his attacking the band and clamping his jaws shut on the ewe's mouth.

"He didn't show any fear at all?" Cady asked Nazario for the second time. "It's important that I know that for my report."

"Not a sign, Doc," said Nazario. "He went right past me like I wasn't there. Then he went straight to the ewe and grabbed her, first by the wool, and when the wool came loose in his mouth, he went for her throat and got her mouth instead."

"He didn't even snap at you?"

"No," said Nazario. "But he cut Michel's dog on the nose when the little collie jumped him."

"I better look at the cut." The veterinarian turned his attention back to the dead coyote and made a clucking sound as he did so. "It's too bad his head is smashed."

"I had to do it," Nazario protested. "It's the only way I could tear him loose. Ask Michel there. He saw it all."

Michel, whose grasp of English was still uncertain, turned to Lorda, who translated the veterinarian's question from English to Basque.

Michel nodded his head emphatically and said in Basque, "We would have had to use an ax to break his hold."

13

"What's so important about the coyote's head?" asked Lorda.

"The laboratory in Reno will need it to examine the coyote's brains, or what's left of them," Cady said. "They're the only ones who can tell us what we're up against here."

"Are you trying to say it's rabies?" asked Lorda.

"I'm not equipped to answer that," said Doctor Cady. "I don't have the facilities in Carson City." He rose and stood staring down at the coyote. "I'll be frank with you. From everything I've read, he showed all the classic signs. But I've never come face-to-face with rabies."

"What signs?"

"His staggering, for one thing. No fear of your herders for another. Coyotes are afraid of man. The most important sign is his fastening onto the ewe's mouth. On the ewe we looked at, you saw the crusted slobber the coyote put on the ewe's mouth. That's not good."

"But a ewe can't get rabid," Lorda argued. "She can't bite anyone or anything."

"No, but she can be a carrier in case a dog bites her."

"Holy Jesus," said Lorda. "What else?"

The veterinarian put his hands in front of him. "Let's don't jump to conclusions until we hear from the lab. It could be something entirely different. Just a crazy coyote, for one thing."

"That's what I said in the first place," said Lorda.

"Well, we'll find out," said Doctor Cady. "Have one of your herders take off the head. Bury the rest of him deep so your dogs or something wild don't dig him up for meat." Taking off his gloves, he added, "And for God's sake, tell your herders and cowboys to wear gloves until I say the word. A rabid animal's blood can get into a cut or a bruise and infect a human."

"What if it *is* rabies, and a man gets bit?"

"He could be a dead man if we don't get to him in time,"

Cady said. "But there are exceptions. I'm talking too much." He strode in the direction of the ranch house. "Tell your men to put the head in a canvas sack for me, not burlap, with holes in it." He said to Lorda, "You owe me breakfast. A Basque omelet will be all I'll charge you."

"Come and get it," said Lorda, lightening his mood.

CHAPTER 5

T he sorrel mare's ears suddenly cocked forward, her nostrils flared, and she came to a dead stop.

"What's the matter, Sassy?" said Tex, surprised. "It's only an old bull we're after. You know his ways, always wandering off."

The tracks they had followed from Pete Lorda's meadowland led between two large granite formations that flanked the trail. The bull's outsize tracks were clearly visible in the moist earth still dampened by the last melting snow of winter. It was not an unfamiliar trail. Tex had explored it time and time again, following the bull's periodic forays away from Pete Lorda's herd of cattle grazing in the ranch's domain. There was no earthly reason the saddle horse would so suddenly act up. Tex touched his spurs lightly against the horse's belly. "Come on," he said in a firm tone. "We haven't got all day."

What happened next was sudden and beyond Tex's comprehension. A tawny mountain lion, his four feet spread out, was springing from his perch on top of one of the rock formations beside the trail. Tex took one look and rammed his spurs into his horse's sides. The sorrel shot out from under the shadow of the springing lion, and Tex ducked forward over the saddle horn. The lion's talons missed him, but not his horse. The beast managed to scrape and bite the mare's rump.

Tex looked backward over his shoulder. The lion had landed on the trail and was twirling in pursuit of man and horse.

In full gallop, Tex could still think to himself, *This is the craziest thing I ever heard of, being chased by a goddam lion.* Because it was not his habit to arm himself when he rode out to check the cattle herd, he had shrugged aside the thought of taking along a saddle carbine. That thought had been inspired by Nazario the sheepherder's encounter with the loco coyote.

The second time Tex looked back, the lion was stumbling from exhaustion. Tex slowed his horse to a lope and circled back toward the ranch. Lorda needed to know what had happened, and the lion had to be hunted down before he killed any of the calves or steers. Tex did not return to the worn trail until he was well along his way through sagebrush country. Even then, he kept the sorrel in a slow, ground-eating lope. When he reached the ranch, he saw Lorda crossing the yard in front of the ranch house and gave out a shrill Texas yell. Lorda heard him and turned around to wait for him. The expression on his face said he was irritated at the sight of the lathered cow horse.

"A loco coyote and now a crazy mountain lion," said Lorda as he heard Tex out. "What are things coming to out here?" He thought for a while, then said, "You're right. We better hunt that thing down before he does damage to the stock."

Within an hour, preparations for hunting the lion had been made. Tex had scraped the lather from his mare and washed the bite and slashes with lye and water, then saddled up a fresh horse. Lorda had taken out his big buckskin gelding and then in afterthought had gone to find Grant, who doubled as tracker for missing livestock.

"Grant will find that troublemaker, you can bet on that," he told Tex.

When they left the ranch, all three riders were armed with saddle carbines.

When they had ridden within sight of the high rock formation from which the mountain lion had leaped, Lorda reined up. He was a cautious man whose nature did not approve of taking unnecessary chances.

"Grant," he said to the Indian tracker, "you check out that rock on foot. You know how to do that better than Tex or me. I don't want that animal jumping down on any of us."

"Okay, boss," said Grant, swinging down from his saddle and handing his reins to Tex. Pulling his carbine from its saddle scabbard, he checked to make sure there was a cartridge in the breech. Then he melted like a shadow into the sagebrush element to which he had been born.

"Lord, he moves quiet," said Tex.

"That's where he comes from, the sagebrush," said Lorda, pulling his own carbine out of its scabbard and crossing it on the saddle in front of him. Tex followed suit, and the two quieted their horses and waited with their eyes fixed on the rock promontory above. Lorda saw movement on the rock and raised his carbine, but it was the Indian who appeared on the ledge.

"This is his home, all right," Grant called down. "Bones and droppings all over." He vanished from sight and in a few minutes materialized out of the sagebrush.

"I better go first," he said when he stood beside them. "I can see his tracks on the trail."

Bent almost double, he studied the ground in front of him. After a few hundred yards, he straightened and waited for Lorda and Tex. "This is where he gave up chasing Tex and took a rest." Grant pointed to the trail ahead. "He started moving again. I think he was heading for the meadow where the bull likes to go."

"I hope to hell he didn't kill the bull," said Tex.

"No danger," said Lorda. "That bull is too big for a lion, I don't care how crazy he is."

Grant had come to a halt at the outskirts of the patch of meadow grass. "This you got to see," he called back. "You'll never see it again."

Lorda and Tex rode to where Grant was standing, looking out upon the little meadow. It was a moment before they could bring themselves to believe what they were seeing.

The torn and ripped body of the mountain lion lay stretched out dead at the feet of the bull. The bull's head was bloody, but he was snorting, very much alive and angry.

"What do you think happened?" Lorda said aloud.

Grant had been examining the body of the lion. "I think this—the lion, crazy he had to be, jumped the bull from in front. The bull hooked him up on his horns, scraped him off, and stomped the hell out of him."

Lorda nodded. "That's what it looks like, all right."

Tex had ridden close to the bull and was inspecting his lacerated head. "He got the hell chewed out of him first."

The three men stood for a while, reconstructing the battle in their minds. Lorda sighed. "I guess we should cut off that cat's head for the doc, but I got no stomach for it. Let's take our bull home and doctor him."

Tex circled the angry bull warily and forced him onto the trail. They left the mountain lion lying where he was. Overhead, the buzzards were already beginning to circle.

Leaving his big buckskin horse for Grant to unsaddle and grain, Pete Lorda set out determinedly for the house. It had taken all three men to rope down the bull once he was in a corral. They scrubbed his bloodied head with lye and water and strong sheep-dip at considerable risk, then pacified him with grain.

Marie was waiting for her father on the front porch. "You got back just in time," she said to Lorda. "Doctor Cady's on the line."

Lorda stopped only to kiss her on the cheek, then went into the ranch house and picked up the black receiver dangling from the telephone on the wall. He looked as though he were expecting the worst.

"I don't have good news, Pete," the grave voice of the veterinarian intoned. "I'll give it to you straight. The lab tells me that coyote's brains were thick with the rabies virus. He was a walking deathtrap."

Lorda swore. "So what do we do now?"

"I've written down a list of do's and don'ts," said Cady. "Get your men together right after breakfast tomorrow. I'll give them a lecture on rabies and what it can do to a range outfit."

"All right, Doc, they'll be here in the house." Lorda was about to withhold the news about the mountain lion until the next morning, then decided to tell the veterinarian now. He spelled out the day's happenings.

"Good Lord!" said Cady. "Things are moving fast. Did you get that cat's head?"

"No."

"Well, do it and quick," said Cady. "Send Tex out with a hatchet and a shovel. I hope the coyotes haven't chewed on that carcass. If they have, there'll be hell to pay."

"Done," said Lorda, then remembered to ask, "What the hell do we do about the ewe whose mouth got chewed up? She dropped twins this morning."

The veterinarian's voice was firm. "You're gonna have to cut her throat, Pete," he said. "She's as good as dead already."

Pete Lorda's voice dropped. "What about her lambs? They been feeding on her milk all day."

The veterinarian considered. "I think they'll be all right.

But unless you can jacket them to a ewe who has lost her lambs, they're going to have to be bottle-fed."

"What about the bull? He's pretty well clawed up around his head."

"Damn!" said Cady. "I don't know. Let me read up on it tonight."

Lorda was about to hang up, then remembered how the coyote had cut Michel's border collie.

The veterinarian paused, then said hesitantly, "You'll probably have to shoot him, too. But let me look at him again. Michel can put him on a chain for now. But for Christ's sake, tell him to watch how that little dog acts."

"Anything else?"

"Not for now," Cady said. "The government people will have to send a warning out to all the ranchers in the area."

"This is a party line," said Lorda wryly. "They all know now." There were sudden bursts of laughter and exclamations along the party line. Pete Lorda could not join in the merriment. He was a worried man.

CHAPTER 6

Doctor Cady was not sure how much of what he was saying was getting through to Pete Lorda's ranch crew, especially the Basque herders whose command of English was uncertain.

He had explained to them that the state hygienic laboratory in Reno had examined the dead coyote. Despite its crushed head, they had found enough solid brain matter to make a scientific test. These tests had conclusively shown the presence of rabies.

Pete Lorda's crew of three sheepherders, two cowboys, and Grant the Indian handyman lined the long table in Mama Lorda's kitchen, nursing coffee that she had prepared for them. Nazario, Ramon, and Michel, the sheepherders, were dressed alike—khaki work shirts, worn and patched Levi's jeans, and wool-lined denim jackets worn-out at the elbows. They had taken off their short-brimmed Stetson hats out of deference to Mama Lorda and Marie, but Slim and Tex, the cowboys, had merely tipped back their wide-brimmed hats in their own manner. A cowboy was rarely seen without his hat, and only Mama Lorda's autocratic insistence had made Slim and Tex remove theirs at the dinner table. But they insisted on keeping their spurs on. When they shuffled their feet, the spurs jangled.

"The rabies virus gets into the animal's bloodstream, then it travels directly to the brain, where it pools," Doctor Cady went on. "Then it spreads through the whole body." The word *virus* made no registry upon the men, and the veterinarian had to be satisfied by describing it as "a big, dangerous germ."

"Ain't there any medicine to stop it from spreading?" Pete Lorda asked.

"There isn't and there is," said Doctor Cady. "A Frenchman name of Pasteur has developed a preventative treatment, but it has to be taken before the symptoms begin to show up. If it isn't, the victim—animal or human—usually dies within a week. With some exceptions."

The men at the table were incredulous. "You can't tell me I'll die from some little animal bite," said Tex the cowboy. "I've been bitten by dogs from the time I was a kid."

"But never by a rabid dog," Doctor Cady retorted. "If you were, you probably wouldn't be here to tell about it."

Tex grumbled in obvious disbelief, but he decided to keep his mouth shut.

Cady's voice became strident. "I can't impress upon you enough that anyone or anything that contracts rabies could die within a week or two. Unless treatment is started immediately."

"What's the treatment?" Lorda asked.

"Fourteen to twenty-four shots of the Pasteur serum, in the stomach," said Cady. "It won't be much fun, but it will save a man's life."

The men accepted the news in varying degrees of belief. "How can we know if something is rabid?" said Tex.

"Normal is the sure clue," said Doctor Cady. "Like the coyote Nazario killed. Coyotes don't attack man. They're afraid of man. They stay as far away from humans as they can, you all know that. But that coyote wasn't afraid of anything with two legs. If Nazario had gotten in his way, the coyote would have bitten him. Take the mountain lion that jumped Tex. Mountain lions, too, stay away from man. They don't go around attacking people, unless they've got rabies."

"What else?" asked Lorda.

Tristant anticipated the veterinarian. "In New Mexico, the herder who died got bit by his own dog."

"See, that wasn't normal," said Cady. "If a dog attacks his owner, he's got to be rabid." The veterinarian spread his hands. "Anything out there that doesn't act normal is probably rabid.

"If one of you gets bitten and doesn't tell anyone, he'll show signs," Cady continued. "A headache first. Can't sleep. His voice gets hoarse. He can't swallow. All these things."

"Then what?" Pete Lorda asked heavily.

"If he's unlucky, he probably dies," said Doctor Cady. "There's no cure for rabies." The doctor hesitated. "But there have been cases where a man lives through it with the serum."

The room fell silent. Pete Lorda knew that each man was exploring in his mind what he would have to do. "You better start carrying guns," Lorda said. "Anything that acts crazy, shoot it." He hesitated, as if realizing the weight of what he was going to say. "Even your dogs."

"And Nazario and Ramon will try to herd a thousand sheep and lambs without a dog that's been trained?" said Tristant sarcastically.

"I'll find new ones somewhere," said Lorda without conviction.

The gathering disbanded in silence.

Unmoving, his shoulders stooped, Pete Lorda said to the veterinarian, "How bad will it get?"

"Pete," said the veterinarian with feeling. "I can't tell you, because I haven't come up against anything like this before. It could spread like wildfire. We're talking epidemic."

CHAPTER 7

When the others had gone, Pete Lorda stood on his front porch with his arms crossed, pondering his situation. *In one week, I lose a good merino ewe,* he said to himself. *I could stand to lose a prize bull, a good saddle horse, and a trained border collie. And if what the doc says about an epidemic is true, this is only the beginning.*

The unfairness of it weighed heavily upon him. He had worked hard to get to where he was. He had come from the Basque provinces of France as a young man not yet twenty. He had done his lonely servitude in the deserts and mountains of Nevada for ten years, paying back the passage money from France to Nevada to his sheepman sponsor, living like an animal against brutal work and awful loneliness, taking his pay in sheep instead of wages, starting off on his own with only a few hundred head of sheep, building his herd off the sale of lambs and wool, buying grazing land instead of depending upon the public domain, putting a house and barns and corrals on it, going back to the Basque Country for a wife who was willing to work as hard as he, and bearing at last a daughter to start a progeny of his own in the New World.

He had wanted sons, but his wife could not bear any more children, so he had sent home for a young Basque of good family to take on the duties of a son. The young man, Michel, had worked out well so far, but time would tell. He had not counted on the budding romance between his daughter and the young Basque. But time would tell whether that was a good thing, too. Michel was learning American ranch ways, including English, for which he was taking lessons from Marie. Marriage had not even been mentioned. Marie was as stern a judge of people as her father, and Michel would have to prove himself before Marie would consent to anything.

The outfit Pete Lorda had built was his life, and now it was threatened. Well, he would fight it with his own weapons.

As if she understood what was going through her father's mind, Marie came out onto the porch and took his work-hardened hand into her own. "Things will work out, Papa," she said. "You've won against worse things than this."

Pete Lorda put his arm around her shoulders. "You are right, little one," he said. "We will win over this trouble, too. Or die trying."

Michel crossed the yard between the ranch house and the bunkhouses and approached them hesitantly. A red flush mantled his cheeks when his eyes met Marie's. She smiled. "Don't be bashful, Michel. I'm not going to bite you."

"I have to talk to your father," Michel said haltingly.

"But you want to talk man-to-man?" said Lorda. Michel nodded. Laughing at his discomfiture, Marie went back into the ranch house.

"Go ahead," said Lorda.

"I don't know what to do about my little collie," said Michel. "I don't want to shoot him."

"It's too early to think about that," said Lorda. "Just keep an eye on him to see if he starts acting funny. That's all we can do for now."

"Well, he's not drinking his water."

Lorda grunted. "That's not good. Try giving him milk. It might go down easier." When Michel turned to go back to the corrals, Lorda added, "You better tie him up at night. Don't take a chance. That's all we need, a sheepherder with rabies."

Michel snapped his fingers in a signal for the little border collie to come to him. The dog eyed him quizzically, but instead of coming to Michel, he backed up to the length of his chain. His ears were cocked forward, and his lips curled back in the beginning of a snarl.

Michel refused to take the dog's action seriously. In a reprimanding voice, he began to approach the dog. He had taken only a few steps when the dog's warning snarl broke his silence, and he leaped forward to attack Michel. At the last instant before the dog bit him, Michel propelled himself backward. The dog struck the end of the chain and stopped there, raging.

Tristant the old sheepherder had come out on the stoop of the bunkhouse in time to see the border collie's lunging attack on his master. Michel had thrown himself backward onto the dirt. "*A la Jinkoa,*" Michel exclaimed in Basque. "I can't believe it."

"You better stay away from him," said Tristant.

"But he let me feed him only last night," said Michel. "I gave him milk, and he took it."

"That was yesterday," said Tristant. "But not today. They say the rabies moves awful fast when it gets started."

"He'll get over it," Michel persisted. "I just got to give him time to get well."

"You heard what the doc told us," Tristant said sternly. "If an animal don't act normal, he could be rabid. There's no getting well. Your dog is as good as dead."

"I don't believe it," said Michel.

"Well, go on fooling yourself," said Tristant. "If you want to see your dog die suffering, it's your animal."

Tex the cowboy had come out of the bunkhouse. He took one look at Michel's dog and said, "If you don't shoot him, I will. I'm not taking a chance on him getting loose and biting me."

"Nobody shoots my dog," said Michel angrily. "If it comes to that, I will do the shooting."

"It will come to that, young man," said Tristant.

"We'll see," said Michel, and stepped closer to the dog. Hunching down on his knees, he began to talk to the border collie in soft tones. After a few minutes, the dog stopped snarling and cocked his ears to listen.

"What did I tell you?" said Michel. "He will get well."

Tex spat angrily into the dirt. "It's your funeral," he said, and walked off in the direction of the horse corral.

"Tristant, what should I do?" Michel asked.

"I don't know what to tell you, Michel," said Tristant. He's acting all right now, but there's no telling how long it will last. Maybe he'll get well. But you can't take a chance. Keep him on that chain. Talk to him if you want to, but don't get close to him. You'll be asking for big trouble if you do." He moved toward the sheep corral. "I got to get to work. The lambs are dropping fast now." On his way, he picked up his long shepherd's crook.

There was work to be done in the busy time of lambing. Michel went inside the bunkhouse to put on his denim jumper and get his gloves. When he passed the border collie again, he called out to him, "Be good now. I got to get to work, too."

The border collie retreated to the end of his chain, snarling.

"Shut up," Michel said angrily in Basque. "*Shilik!*" He was losing his patience with the dog, but he still could not accept the idea of shooting him.

CHAPTER 8

Ramon had brought his sheep into bed-ground early for two reasons. The first was that he did not want to leave himself exposed in the open if a rabid coyote were to attack him. The second was that he wanted to build a barrier, crude though it may be, around his tepee tent for the night. He had chopped a dozen or more tall bitterbrushes and dug their roots into the ground around the tent. Only the entrance was exposed, and there would be a cookfire burning there to scare off any coyote.

Ramon was a sheepherder who took life seriously. Ever since the veterinarian's lecture, an inordinate fear had been growing in Ramon. From the moment he left the home ranch with his band of yearlings, he had carried his carbine through every waking moment. The first day out on the range had been a nightmare of imagined coyotes circling his sheep and him. Ramon knew they were out there somewhere, but he did not know where or how many. He had drawn the veterinarian aside to ask him whether he knew if there were many or few, and Doctor Cady had told him frankly, "Nobody knows how many coyotes are out there, but from all the reports that have come to me over the years, I would say there's a hundred or more."

"That's impossible," said Ramon. "I've only seen a dozen in my time herding sheep here."

"Well, we'll soon find out," said Doctor Cady. "If there's rabies loose out there, they'll show up. If they're sick, they won't be afraid of a man or his gun. And what about the lions and the wildcats? We can't disregard them."

"So what am I supposed to do?" Ramon asked.

"Shoot and shoot and shoot," said Cady, "and hope they die of the disease in a hurry."

Ramon ate his dinner early and quickly, huddling over his little cookfire while the flames seared his lamb chops and potatoes. The sheep bedded down quietly, and his shaggy sheepdog and his pack burro did not seem alarmed. That set Ramon's mind at ease, and he allowed himself the time to roll and smoke a cigarette and take a long jet of wine from his gourd.

When he was done, he bent down to bank the fire. A spitting blur of movement came out of the night, struck him on the shoulder, and bounded inside his tent. The force of the intruder's blow had knocked Ramon on his backside. Bewildered, he scrambled to his feet and stared into the tent. It was a bobcat gone crazy, leaping against the walls of the tent and being bounced back. Ramon dropped to his knees and groped for his carbine. But there was no need for it. The bobcat screeched once and bounded over Ramon's body into the night. Ramon wheeled on his knees and pointed the muzzle of the gun in a semicircle.

When he realized that the bobcat was not coming back, he sat back on his haunches and frantically examined his shoulder. There was neither blood nor even a tear in his Levi's jacket. The bobcat had missed him completely.

When his nerves had quieted, Ramon sat down on one of his burro's pack bags, rolled a cigarette, and reached for his wine gourd. There was serious thinking to do and a decision to be made.

Ramon awakened with the first gray light of dawn, picked up his gun, and went outside to survey his band of sheep. They were just beginning to stir.

He built a cookfire and made his coffee in the fire-blackened coffeepot resting on the hairpin-shaped cooking iron over the flames. When the coffeepot boiled over through its spout, he poured cold water into it from his canteen to settle the grounds.

While the coffee was boiling, Ramon had opened his bread sack and cut himself a huge chunk out of the sourdough loaf. Pouring a full measure of coffee into his oversize tin cup, Ramon sweetened the brew with canned milk and sugar. The coffee, steaming in the cold air of dawn, gave him back confidence and strength. Needing even more strength, he cut himself another chunk of sourdough bread and dipped it into the tin cup. When the cup was empty and his belly warm, Ramon picked up his carbine and whistled for his dog. Cutting directly through the waking sheep, he went to where he guessed the trouble and noise had come from while he was in bed. In normal times, Ramon would have gone out to the sheep as soon as he heard the thudding of hooves, but not now when there was danger waiting for him in the night.

His little sheepdog whimpered and then growled, and Ramon knew they had found the place where the trouble had happened in the night. He found a dead ewe with her throat cut and stared down at her. There was no way of telling if the coyote that had killed the ewe was rabid, but he guessed the chances were likely.

In any case, Ramon had made up his mind. He started his band of sheep on their direction for the day, but it was not according to plan. He was pointed back toward the home ranch, not toward the Sierra that was to be his destination. Ramon set about arranging his camp and loading the burro with its pack bags and his canvas bed tied on top.

Before he set out to follow the sheep, there was an interruption. A coyote appeared on the ridge, totally ignoring a human presence. In plain view, the coyote made his wavering way in the direction of the sheep. It was the easiest of shots. Ramon raised his carbine and knocked down the coyote. To make sure of his suspicions, Ramon walked to where the coyote was lying and examined him. The bullet had caught him high on the shoulder, but Ramon was not interested in that. He was regarding the white froth that outlined the coyote's mouth. That told the sheepherder all he wanted to know.

Crossing the yard, Pete Lorda saw the dust before he saw the band of sheep that was raising it.

"What now?" he asked aloud and climbed up on the corral fence to have a better look. As he suspected, it was Ramon with the yearling band. By this time, they should have been ten miles along the route to the foothills of the Sierra.

Ramon was in no hurry. He was giving the yearlings all the time they needed to feed through the white sage that surrounded the home ranch. When Ramon's dusty silhouette came into view, Pete Lorda could see that he was not carrying his carbine slung over his shoulder, but in his hands. Lorda climbed down from the fence and went to meet the sheepherder.

When they were facing each other, Lorda said, "What are you doing back here?"

"I quit," said Ramon.

Lorda regarded him incredulously, but the expression on Ramon's dark Mexican face was of a man who had absolutely made up his mind.

"What are you saying?" said Lorda. "You're not making sense."

"Let me tell you what I'm saying," said Ramon. He related his encounters with the bobcat and the coyote who was going to attack the band of sheep before Ramon shot him. "I am not going out there again," said Ramon. "Only a crazy man would herd sheep in country filled with rabid coyotes."

Pete Lorda threw up his hands in helplessness. "Where does that leave me?"

"Send Michel out with the yearlings," said Ramon. "It's about time he got his feet wet."

"He doesn't know the range," said Lorda. "With the snows there in the Sierra, I haven't had a chance to show him."

"How about Tristant?"

"He's too old," said Lorda. "I can't trust him to keep strong young yearlings together. He's just right where he is now, looking after the lambs until their mothers take them."

Ramon understood without Lorda telling him that Lorda was also making sure that old Tristant had a home and a little work in his old age. He relented.

"I don't know what to tell you to do," said Ramon. "When Nazario's lambs are ready to go out on the range with their mothers, there will be hell to pay. Those coyotes will kill them like rabbits."

"You don't have to tell me," said Lorda. "But I got to do something." He paused in thought, then snapped his fingers. "I have an idea. We all got to talk to see if it will work. Unload your burro, but don't pack yourself up. I'll send Michel to round up the others. We'll meet in the ranch house."

CHAPTER 9

P ete Lorda's face was gray with worry and fatigue when he faced his ranch crew across the long wooden table in the ranch house kitchen. The lambs in Nazario's band had been dropping at a rapid rate now that the lambing time had come, and Lorda had spent a sleepless night helping Nazario and the old shepherd Tristant deliver the lambs. He had gone from ewe to ewe with his kerosene lantern, watching to see if the birthing was going well. More than once, he had to work his hands inside a mother's belly to straighten a lamb that was caught crosswise in its delivery. His hands knew instinctively what they were doing, and he was famous for his skill at delivering lambs in trouble, and in the bargain, saving the mother's life. It was hard and nervously demanding labor, and his lean unshaven face reflected his worry.

Now, his worries were trebled with Ramon's decision to quit. While Michel was rounding up the crew, Lorda had made two quick calls. One was to the Santa Fe Hotel in Reno, where

Basque sheepherders spent their time off between jobs at one of the numerous sheep outfits in the deserts and mountains of western Nevada. He had had no luck in finding a herder and had not expected to. It was lambing season, and the sheep outfits needed every man they could get their hands on.

Lorda's second call had been to the veterinarian. The news was even worse there. Meeker, the sheepman whose range spread was next to Lorda's, had already been hit five times by rabid coyotes, and the sheep outfits on the other side of Lorda were hurting, too.

Doctor Cady's premonition of an epidemic in the making was coming true.

"We're in trouble," Lorda said to his men, "but I got an idea that could save us. I'm talking about cowboys on horseback, cowboys who are good shots with both pistols and rifles." Lorda addressed Ramon directly. "Ramon, would you go back out with the yearlings if there was a sharpshooter circling the band all day?"

"I don't know," said Ramon. "It's worth thinking about."

"Nazario?"

"I like it," said Nazario. "A man on horseback can get to a coyote in a hurry, a lot faster than I can."

"We've left out our cowboys," said Lorda, smiling now that his plan was taking shape. "What do you two think about it?"

Slim and Tex looked at each other. "It sounds crazy, but it just might work," said Tex. "We pack up and go with a sheep-herder and spend our days circling the band and getting in some target practice."

"Who's going to take care of feeding the cattle and the ranch horses?" Slim asked.

Pete Lorda waved the question aside. "That I can take care of, and Michel can help me."

Michel shook his head in wonder. "When I was a boy in the Basque Country, I dreamed about being a cowboy," he grinned.

"Now you can wear a big cowboy hat," said Lorda. He got

to his feet. "Well, we are agreed, anyway. We'll see what happens. There can't be that many coyotes out there."

"I don't know," said Ramon, remembering what Doctor Cady had said. "We could be in for a big surprise."

As much out of curiosity as duty, Ramon did not even bother to unpack his burro. Telling himself that he would go along with Pete Lorda's plan for a day or two, he held the band of yearlings in place. He waited until he saw Tex emerging from the horse corral. The claw marks on his sorrel mare were still bleeding, and Tex was riding Big Red, a saddle horse with proven endurance. Tex kept his horse at a trot until he caught up. He looked ready for action, his waist encircled by a cartridge belt and a holstered revolver, and his saddle carbine ready in his scabbard.

He reined to a stop when he reached Ramon. "All right, where do you want me?" he asked.

"In the lead ahead of the sheep," said Ramon. "That way, you can shoot without your bullets coming my way. And my sheeps' way, most of all."

Tex pulled his revolver out of its holster and twirled its cylinder to check the load. "Okay," he said. "I'm loaded for bear. This is new duty for me, but I think I'm going to like it."

When Tex had trotted away in the right direction, Ramon whistled to his shaggy sheepdog, Barbo. The dog made a circling pass at the rear of the band, banking as he went. In a moment, the yearling band was on its way along the grazing route it would hold for the next few weeks on Lorda's allotted land. Ramon followed in the ground-eating stride of the sheepherder, but his head was raised in anticipation of what he hoped was going to happen.

Ramon did not have long to wait. It was midmorning when the shots sounded, one singly and then two in a pair. Ramon surmised that Tex had missed on his first shot, closed in on his target, and scored with his next two shots.

When the sheep had settled down from the crack of the pistol shots, Ramon pushed the band forward until he caught up with Tex. The cowboy had swung off his saddle and was inspecting a dark object at his feet. As Ramon expected, it was a dead coyote.

"That's number one," said Tex. "Look at that saliva around his mouth."

"By God," said Ramon. "I think Lorda's idea is going to turn out good. I feel better already."

"Do we have to bury the sonofabitch?"

Ramon shook his head. "Leave him for the buzzards."

Tex reloaded his pistol with two of the .45-caliber bullets in his belt. He had scarcely time to holster the pistol when Ramon gave a sharp cry. Tex turned to look where Ramon was pointing. A coyote had come in from the side and was fastened onto a ewe. Tex swung into his saddle and ran his horse through the band of sheep, scattering them to right and left, to reach the flailing ewe. Tex rode to the scene and shot the coyote. The ewe pulled loose from the coyote's grasp, but her throat was bloody.

When Ramon reached the scene, Tex said, "Am I supposed to kill the ewe, too? She will get rabies for sure."

"No," said Ramon in instant decision. "Let her go," he said. "There's no way for me to tell whether she is infected or not. If she is, she will be dead in a week. If she isn't, all the better for Lorda."

The yearlings had scattered from the noise and the commotion. Ramon set about rounding them up into one band. "Two in one day," he called back to Tex. "Good shooting."

CHAPTER 10

Ｗith the end of the sheephook, Michel edged the tin saucer of milk closer to the border collie. The dog eyed it curiously, but when he raised his head to look at Michel, his lips curled into a snarl. Michel did not move. He stayed on his knees with the sheephook held in one hand. The collie's ears were cocked forward, keyed to the man.

Marie had come down from the ranch house in jeans and boots to watch Michel's overtures to the border collie, but Michel had ordered her to stay behind the protection of the sturdy corral fence.

"You got to protect yourself," he said sternly. "When he jumps, it's fast as lightning."

"I know dogs," said Marie defensively. "I've been raised with sheepdogs."

"But not crazy ones," said Michel. "Come on, puppy. Drink your milk."

The dog seemed to respond to Michel's gentle voice. He inched forward to the saucer, his nostrils quivering.

"He's hungry," said Marie. "He's awfully thin, Michel."

"I know," said Michel. "It hurts me to look at him."

"He won't take any food at all?" said Marie. "I can go get some meat scraps from Mama's kitchen."

"All right, let's try it," said Michel. So far, the dog had eaten nothing. Michel remained on his knees, talking to the border collie in a soothing tone.

Unexpectedly, the little dog plunged his muzzle into the bowl of milk. His efforts to lap were in vain, and the milk dribbled out of the corners of his mouth. But he swallowed, not once but twice. Michel could have shouted for joy, but he restrained himself.

The old sheepherder Tristant had been watching from the bunkhouse stoop where he was smoking his curved old pipe. "A la Jinkoa," he muttered. "You might make it with him after all. But I tell you, be careful. Don't get too sure of yourself and get bitten."

Marie's boots scuffed on the hard-packed earth. The border collie leaped back in alarm to the end of his chain, snarling furiously. Marie watched Michel's face fall and knew she had interrupted something important. She looked questioningly at Michel.

"It's all right," said Michel. "He was drinking, and some of it was staying down."

Marie proffered the plate of meat scraps over the fence. "Maybe he'll eat, too."

"At least we can try," said Michel. He took a meaty bone and tossed it gently to the young collie. The dog leaped backward, as though something hurtful had been thrown at him.

They watched in silence until the young dog's nostrils began to twitch at the smell of food. "By gosh," Marie exclaimed. "At least he knows it's food."

After a wait, the collie edged closer to the bone. Michel and Marie looked at each other expectantly. "He might take it," Marie whispered.

The collie did. He tore loose a morsel of fat from the bone, chewed it, and then spit it up chokingly.

They moaned in unison, but Tristant comforted them. "The important thing is that he took the meat," he said. "Maybe next time he'll keep it down."

Marie came through the corral gate, her face animated with pride. She grasped Michel's hand. "Tristant is right," she said. "I know he's going to get well."

But at the excitement in her voice, the dog retreated to the end of his chain again, his mouth curled in a snarl. Michel was not paying attention to him. He was staring down at Marie's hand clasping his. It was the first time they had touched.

Michel raised his eyes to Marie's face. "*Agur,* Marie," he said shyly in Basque.

Marie did not pull her hand away from his. "Hello to you, too, Michel," she responded softly.

The dog was forgotten. From the stoop where he sat smoking his curved pipe, Tristant smiled warmly. He muttered to himself, "At least something good is coming out of all this trouble."

Pete Lorda had been watching the interlude from the big window in the ranch house. "Something's happening between those two," he said in Basque to Mama Lorda working at the kitchen stove.

Without turning around, Mama Lorda said, "She could do worse."

"But Michel doesn't know anything," said Lorda. "He doesn't know the range. He speaks good English now, but he doesn't know business. He doesn't even know the worth of a good merino ewe. The Americans will eat him alive."

"They didn't eat you alive."

"But it was different then. The range was open land. I could work for sheep instead of wages. That time is over with."

"He can learn if he works for you," said Mama Lorda. "Give him time. He'll learn what he has to learn from you. Who knows? Maybe he can be a partner in time." She paused. "All that's not important compared to what he is inside. He's a good boy."

Lorda laughed. "We're forgetting about Marie. She isn't exactly without boyfriends. Meeker's son is hot on her trail, and he would be a good catch. The family's outfit is right next to ours."

"That family's not impressed with Basques. His mother doesn't come over for coffee three times a year. And when she does, she tries to put me down for my bad English. If Marie were to marry into that family, we would never see her."

"Ed Meeker doesn't try putting me down," said Lorda heatedly. "He tried it once, but never again."

"That's because you are as big a sheepman as he is," said Mama Lorda. "Money in sheep and land is all that matters with him."

"You're too hard on him. He's been a good neighbor."

"That's because he's practical," said Mama Lorda. "He would earn nothing by making trouble for you."

"Maybe you're right," said Lorda. "Anyway, we've both got a big handful of trouble on our hands now. I don't like the looks of this at all. If this rabies comes to be an epidemic, we're going to lose sheep, a lot of sheep. There goes my men's wages, the ranch's expenses. *Jinkoa,*" he swore. "It makes me sick to think about it."

"Well, here comes the cowboy," said Mama Lorda. "Maybe he'll have good news."

Lorda put on his hat, and Mama Lorda kissed him on the cheek. "You worry too much. Don't add Marie to your troubles. She's got enough of both of us in her to take care of herself. Let's wait and see what happens."

Tex had dismounted and was tying his sweating horse, Big Red, to the hitching rail alongside the house. Looking hard at him, Pete Lorda could see no big worry on his face.

"I should be riding herd," said Tex. "But I just had to take a quick run back and tell you how your plan is working out."

"Well?"

"So far, better than we could have hoped. Four coyotes in one day!"

Pete Lorda whistled. "How many yearlings lost?"

"One got chewed up before I could get to her," said Tex. "But she will live if the rabies don't kill her."

"By God, we might have the answer to saving our stock."

"I can't tell you that. Those hills are crawling with coyotes. Doc Cady told Ramon there were hundreds out there. I'm beginning to believe he's right."

"Maybe Slim should go out with you," said Lorda.

Tex shook his head vehemently. "No! This is my show! I'm going to be the champion coyote hunter in Nevada. They'll put me down in the history books."

"Maybe so," Lorda grinned. "Anyway, Slim will be going out with Nazario tomorrow or next day. I want to save those lambs."

Slim was waving from the training corral. Before taking the trail back to Ramon's band of yearlings, Tex stopped to water Big Red and see how Sassy, his wounded mare, was faring. Slim was working a filly on the long lunge line in the training corral. When Tex rode up, Slim stepped out to meet him. His face registered concern.

"I wouldn't go into Sassy's corral right off," said Slim. "She's been acting up all day."

"Acting up how?" asked Tex.

"First, she's off her feed and water," said Slim. "Then she's been chewing on the fence posts."

"She's probably jealous," said Tex. "She got sore yesterday when I saddled up Big Red. But I need a strong horse for riding herd through rough country. Sassy's too delicate for that. She's a cutting horse, after all."

Slim shook his head. "It's worse than that, Tex," he said. "Wait until you see the chunks she's bitten off that fence. Her mouth is bloody."

"Don't tell me she's—" Tex started to say.

"I'm not telling you nothing," said Slim. "I'm no veterinarian. Take a look for yourself."

Tex morosely tied Big Red to the hitching rail at the horse trough. "I've trained that pretty little thing since she was a colt." He strode heavily toward the corral where Sassy had been put while she was being doctored with lye and water and sheep-dip on the deep claw marks the lion had inflicted upon her.

Tex stopped at the corral gate to see for himself what his horse had done to the fence. He was shocked at what he saw. Slim was right. The fence showed a lot more than the usual mild chewing that horses did when they were bored. It was as if Sassy had eaten mouthfuls out of the thick wooden rails of the fence. Her mouth was bloody.

Instead of coming to him when Tex called, Sassy was backed up in a corner of the corral. Her ears were laid back, and she was pawing the ground.

"Holy Jesus!" said Tex.

Nevertheless, he opened the small side gate and stepped into the corral. The instant his back was turned, Sassy came for him. Slim yelled in warning, and Tex threw himself sideway to avoid the rush. Sassy crashed into the gate as if it didn't exist. The impact knocked her to her knees, and Tex vaulted out of the corral while she was still down.

Slim held a hand out to help Tex to his feet. "I would have told you, but she's gotten worse."

"It don't matter, Slim," said Tex. "What counts is whether she's got the rabies or not."

There was the sound of an engine beyond the corrals. It was Doctor Cady in his weathered pickup truck. Tex ran out to the road and waved the veterinarian down.

"God, am I glad to see you," Tex said hoarsely.

Doctor Cady turned off the engine and stepped out of the truck. "Don't tell me," he said. "Your prize horse got infected after all."

"I think so," said Tex. "But I can't tell. Will you look at her?"

Cady walked over to Sassy's corral and saw what she had done to the fence railing. He listened to Slim and Tex tell their accounts of what had happened. He shook his head sadly. "I'm sorry, Tex," he said. "She's sick, all right."

"Can you do anything?"

"I can give her a shot, but I'm telling you right now that it's too late. The symptoms have probably started. If it makes you feel better, let's get on with it. You and Slim are going to have to rope her down so I can give her an injection."

Roping Sassy down was not an easy thing to accomplish, but both cowboys were practiced at it. Each took a lariat from the tack room and came out. Tex cautiously climbed the bottom rungs of the fence and shook out a loop. Farther along the fence, Slim did the same.

When Tex called to his horse, Sassy made the same rush as before. When she was close, Tex threw a loop over her head and pulled it tight. When she was roped, Slim vaulted into the corral and looped her hind legs and, with a fence post as brace, pulled the rope. Sassy flopped to her side on the ground. Doctor Cady squeezed through the gate with a huge hypodermic needle of antiserum in his hand. He thrust it into Sassy's stomach, emptied it, and leaped clear away.

"I gave her as much as the hypo would hold," he said as the

three men stood outside. "I can't promise you anything, Tex," Doctor Cady said. "If the shot works, all to the good. But I'll be frank with you. I think it's too late."

"In which case—" said Tex.

"In which case, she'll be dead in a week, and nothing will stop it. I warned all of you there's no cure once the symptoms get started. And they are well along with Sassy."

The tears did not go well with Tex's hardened face. He turned away quickly. "Well, I've got to get back to Ramon. He'll be a nervous wreck by the time I show up."

When he had mounted Big Red, he called out, "I owe you, Doc," and reined away at a trot.

CHAPTER 11

W arm weather and marking time for the lambs had arrived together, and Pete Lorda's sheep ranch was a beehive of activity.

Lambing was over and done with, and already wether and ewe lambs had taken enough nourishment from their mothers to gambol and cavort in the main corral. Once having taken their mothers' milk, they seemed to grow before one's eyes.

It was time for docking and marking, the busiest time of the sheep year. Shearing by the itinerant Mexican crews would come later, on the eve of the sheep bands' departure for the High Sierra.

Nazario's band of ewes and lambs was being crowded by the sheepdogs into a long wooden chute with a separating gate at the end, shunting the lambs into one corral and the mothers into another.

All the ranch crew except Ramon and Tex, who were herding the yearling band, were occupied in the marking. Pete

Lorda was overseeing the division of duties. Tristant, Michel, Grant the handyman, and even Slim the cowboy took turns in catching the young lambs by hand and positioning them on the marking block for Nazario's docking-and-marking operation. Both ewe and wether lambs had their tails removed and their ears notched. The wether lambs were neatly castrated by Nazario's razor-sharp knife to ensure milder meat for the lamb buyers.

When the operation was done, Michel placed the marked lambs along the fence line until they had recovered enough to return to their mothers in the main corral. Finally, ewes and lambs would be turned out into pasture to wait there until Nazario's band was complete.

Then the dogs would herd another bunch into the chute for the next go-round of separation and marking. The work was long and arduous, with hardly time to eat lunch, which Mama Lorda had brought out to the corrals in big cast-iron Dutch ovens, with a supply of tin plates and wine cups. Throughout the day, Marie brought an oversize coffeepot out for the workers whenever there was a respite in the feverish activity.

By the end of two long days, five hundred lambs had been marked, and Nazario's band of ewes and lambs was ready to move from the ranch. They would be herded into the desert hills sprouting with the first green of spring.

Pete Lorda, standing with Nazario and Slim at the head of the band, was apprehensive.

"Don't waste your bullets on long shots at them coyotes," Lorda said to Slim. "Do like Tex told me he did. Run your horse right at them and shoot point-blank. With a horse, you can outrun them, head them off."

Slim patted the revolver at his hip. "Don't worry. I'm not in the habit of missing, and this old .45 makes big holes."

Pete Lorda's gaze was on the desert hills into which Nazario's band would go. Something was bothering him. "The most important thing is to keep on the move. Keep circling the band. The coyotes know these little lambs are for the taking. One bite, and the lamb is dead. I can't afford to lose any."

Slim was about to say, "You worry too much. Your lambs will be safe. I'm a dead shot." He stopped short when Pete Lorda gave a sudden yell. Slim saw his face contort. He was looking at the rim of desert hills in front of them. Slim wheeled his horse to see what Lorda was staring at.

A ragged line of shaggy coyotes was coming out of the hills toward the band. Pete Lorda gasped in incredulity. He shouted a warning to Nazario, but Nazario had already seen what was coming. He was unslinging the carbine off his shoulder.

"Cut the bastards off," Lorda said to Slim. Slim touched his spurs to his horse and, drawing his revolver, broke into a run to intercept the dark attacking line.

There was nothing else for Pete Lorda to do but run to the ranch house and get his rifle and order Tristant, Grant, and Michel to do the same.

"Stay inside out of trouble's way!" Lorda cried to his wife and Marie. "Don't take a chance on getting bit." He ran to the gun cabinet, grasped his Winchester carbine and loaded it hurriedly, and stuffed a handful of extra cartridges into his coat pocket. When he emerged from the house, Tristant and Michel were waiting for him.

They had climbed to the top of the fence to see what was happening with Nazario's sheep band. The clearing where the band had been waiting was a scene of utter chaos and crashing gunfire. The line of coyotes had reached the band and were darting everywhere, snarling and slashing as they went. Nazario was in among the hysteria-stricken sheep and lambs, thrusting the muzzle of his carbine flush against the coyotes nearest to him. From the head of the band, Slim was spurring his horse from one coyote to another, shooting down at them as he rode.

When Lorda, Tristant, Grant, and Michel joined the turmoil, the gunfire rose to a crescendo.

Then suddenly, the deafening gunfire came to a stop, and all that could be heard was the bleating of ewes and the plaintive crying of the lambs that had been bitten.

His head bowed and his feet dragging, Lorda was weaving through the clearing, counting the dead and wounded sheep and lambs. He did not bother with the coyotes except to kick at their dead bodies as he passed them. It had been a dreadful encounter, and Lorda's expression showed it. Only when the counting was done would he know how much the band had been decimated in the ferocious assault.

The fire pit into which the dead coyotes and sheep were thrown resembled a funeral pyre twenty feet high. The pit had been filled with sagebrush and soaked with kerosene. When the bed of coals was substantial, the men began throwing in the bodies and piling additional sagebrush over them.

Doctor Cady, the veterinarian, was wearing a bandanna across his nose and mouth to ward off the stench of burning wool and hair and meat. "At least there will be a dozen less coyotes to contend with when you move the band into the hills," he said to Lorda. "Better burning than burying. The fire will kill off the rabies virus, too."

"What's going on with the other outfits, like Meeker's?" Lorda asked. "Their ewes and lambs are moving into the hills, too."

"They're hurting," said Doctor Cady. "But not nearly as bad as you. Meeker is using your idea of sending horseback riders with rifles along with his two bands. But it's no easy job finding men who can ride and shoot at the same time. Then, not too many want to take a chance on getting bitten by a rabid animal."

"How long will it go on, this epidemic?"

"As long as there's coyotes up there," said Doctor Cady.

"But the longer it goes on, they'll be dying from the disease as well as getting shot. This can't go on forever."

They fell silent as Tristant and Michel threw two more lambs into the flames. "If it goes on too long, we'll all be broke," said Lorda. "We got to meet expenses, you know."

"I know, Pete," said Doctor Cady. "But there isn't a damned thing I can do about it."

Pete Lorda turned away from the fire and began walking toward the ranch house. When he and Doctor Cady passed the bunkhouses, the doctor stopped. He was watching Michel shoving a pan of milk toward his border collie. Marie was standing by him. "What's going on here?" he asked Lorda.

"Michel thinks the pup will get well," said Lorda. "He's keeping the little dog alive on milk."

"He's fooling himself," said Cady. "But I could be wrong. That little collie should have died by now. Even a veterinarian can't be sure what will live and what will die."

"He's got Marie on his side now," said Lorda. "I'm outnumbered."

Marie sucked in her breath as she watched Michel's hand move closer to the border collie at the end of his chain. The little collie was not snarling. Neither were his lips curled in warning. He stood without moving, his eyes fixed on the approaching hand.

Finally, Marie could stand it no longer. "Michel," she whispered, "he's going to bite you."

Michel withdrew his hand uncertainly. "If he was going to bite me," he said with annoyance, "he would have done it by now."

"Maybe, maybe not," said Marie. "I've got a feeling he will. It's not worth taking the chance. You know what Doctor Cady said. You could die if he bites you."

Doctor Cady and Pete Lorda had come over to watch. "What are you doing, young man?" Cady said angrily.

"I'm curing my pup," said Michel. "He's drinking his milk now."

"That means nothing," said the veterinarian.

"But he hasn't tried to bite me."

"That doesn't mean he won't," said Cady. "I'll show you what I mean." He picked up a stick from the ground and threw it gently at the dog.

The transformation in the border collie was instantaneous. He leaped at the doctor with fangs bared, snarling viciously.

"That's what I mean," Cady said.

"But he hasn't growled at me in over a week," said Michel.

"Stick your hand out to him now," said Cady. "But not close enough that he can bite you."

Michel did as the doctor said. The collie whirled and struck at Michel's hand with the deadly suddenness of a rattlesnake. Michel leaped backward in astonishment.

"Do you see what I mean?" said Cady. "His mind is gone, but not his craftiness. He's just been waiting for the chance to sink his fangs into your hand."

"And then you'll die!" Marie cried out. "What are you trying to prove?"

"That not everything that's bitten has to die," said Michel. "I still think he's going to get well. He would have died by now if he were really rabid."

"I'll grant you that," said Doctor Cady. "Maybe he'll be one of those that live through it. I can't be positive. There's a lot of unknowns about rabies."

"Give me just one more week," said Michel. "If he lives through it, maybe he'll get well."

Cady stiffened. "I'll not be a party to this. You might be right, but I think you'll end up wrong. Just promise me one thing. Don't try again to pet him. It's not worth risking your life."

"All right," said Michel. "I promise." But it was a promise he knew he would not keep.

CHAPTER 12

The massive dose of antiserum that Doctor Cady injected into Sassy had not taken at all. If anything, the sorrel mare was in worse condition than the first time Slim had come to see her.

Her sculptured head looked as though it had been beaten bloody with a club. Her fine nose was crushed, and her front teeth had been broken off. She stood almost splay-footed in the middle of the horse corral, as though she were contemplating how to damage herself further.

Tex was leaning against the fence with Slim. He had ridden back from Ramon's band of sheep to see if the antiserum had worked.

"I can phone the vet and ask him to give her another shot," said Slim.

Tex shook his head morosely. "It won't do no good. She's a goner." He was silent for a long moment, thinking. "Can we just turn her loose out into the desert? She can run until she can't run anymore, and then she'll die out in the open."

"We can't take that chance, Tex," said Slim. "The minute we open that gate, she'll come looking for someone."

"What do you mean?"

"I mean that she's turned killer," said Slim. "Every day when I try to feed her, she comes after me. She just barrels into the fence and tries to climb it to get at me. If we turn her loose, she'll go after the first thing she sees, animal or human."

"Which leaves us with no choice but to shoot her," said Tex slowly.

"That's right," said Slim. "Protect the ranch. Sooner or later, she'll climb out of that corral. Then there'll be hell to pay."

"You're right," said Tex. "But I haven't got it in my heart to shoot her. Hell, I've raised her from a colt. She was the most loving little filly I ever saw."

Slim was silent. "Well, I haven't got much heart for horse killing," he said, as if the words were being dragged out of him. "But I'll do it for you."

"My thanks, Slim," said Tex. "It's a big thing to ask of a friend."

"When do you want me to do the job?"

"Not while I'm here," said Tex. "Wait until I'm on my way back to Ramon's camp."

"Well, you better be on your way," said Slim, "before I change my mind."

Tex pushed himself away from the fence. He stared long and earnestly at his sorrel. "Good-bye, little horse," he said. "We had a good go together. Given time, we would have won a cutting-horse championship along the way."

As if something in Tex's voice had struck a chord in her memory, Sassy nickered. Tex's shoulders slumped in misery. And then Sassy reverted to the disease. She reared up on her hind legs and pawed the sky, neighing shrilly at Slim and Tex. Tex straightened his shoulders and made his way beyond the barn. Without a good-bye, he mounted and spurred Big Red into a trot.

The echo of Slim's shot carried to him as he was working his way up a ravine that would lead him to Ramon's camp. Tex set his face and acted as if he had not heard.

Tex was in no mood for conversation when he reached Ramon's sheep camp. The echo of the shot that had killed Sassy was still sounding in his ears, and his anger had been mounting all the way to the sheep camp.

He dismounted only long enough to pick up his carbine and load it. He also filled the slots in his cartridge belt and made sure that his .45 revolver was loaded. He wanted revenge against all the rabid animals he could find in the jumble of rocks that lay above the camp. Ramon shouted to him from where he was standing watch below on his band of yearlings. Tex acknowledged his call with a short wave of his hand, then mounted and climbed toward the rock formations that resembled the one that had given concealment to the mountain lion that infected Sassy.

Tex's anger and carelessness were to cost him. He was weaving his way through the high rocks and dense bitterbrush when the lynx landed on his shoulders, sank his fangs into the side of his neck, and hung there. The impact almost knocked Tex out of his saddle. He jammed his boots into his stirrups and reached backward to rip the clinging animal loose.

Disgustedly, he threw the lynx to the ground and spurred forward to give himself room to draw his pistol. In the confinement of the rock formations, the shot was so loud that his horse almost leaped out from under him. Tex reined him down and looked back. The big .45 slug had almost blown off the lynx's head. Tex swore in satisfaction, then reached back again to see how badly the lynx had bitten him. His hand came away dripping with blood. Tex stared at his bloody hand and knew panic.

The warnings that Doctor Cady had spelled out for the ranch crew came back to him. Tex put spurs to his horse and headed for Ramon's sheep camp at a dead run. Ramon was there to meet him. "Soap and water!" cried Tex. "I've got to clean out the bite."

"I will do it for you," said Ramon. The washbasin and a canteen of water were set on a stump. Tex ripped off his bloody shirt, and Ramon began to wash out the bite.

"Whiskey," said Tex. "Do you have any whiskey?"

Ramon dug into his pack bag and came up with a pint of whiskey wrapped in a cloth. "Pour it right into the bite," said Tex.

"It will sting you," said Ramon.

"I don't care. I've got to get rid of the infection."

Ramon poured the whiskey into his palm and daubed it on the wound in Tex's shoulder. Tex winced in satisfaction, then reached for the flask and took a big swallow.

"Okay," he gasped. "Now I make tracks for a doctor and some of that serum." He reached into his clothes sack and pulled out a clean shirt.

"You mean you're leaving me alone?" cried Ramon.

"What else can I do?" said Tex. "I don't want to die. Don't lose your head. Lorda will send up someone to take my place."

Ramon paled. "Who can he send? Slim is going out with Nazario's band tomorrow."

"Don't worry," said Tex. "He'll send someone."

"Like hell he will," said Ramon, but his words were drowned out by the hoofbeats of Tex's horse.

While Michel held Tex's head and shoulders under the pump, Grant swabbed and squeezed the bite on Tex's shoulder to make it bleed. When the bite was bled out, Grant poured black sheep-dip on the wound. Tex howled in pain as the burning liquid penetrated the gouges the lynx had made in his flesh.

"If that doesn't clean me out," Tex gasped, "I don't know what will."

Pete Lorda was crossing the yard from the ranch house with long strides. He pulled on his hat as he approached. "We're in luck," he said. "We don't have to go all the way to the hygienic laboratory in Reno. There's a doctor in Carson who's got a supply of rabies vaccine, just in case."

"Can I get my shot today?" said Tex.

"Today and every day for twenty days," said Lorda. Anticipating Tex's question, he said, "You won't have to move into town. You can stay here and drive the pickup in for your shot."

"That's a relief," said Tex. "I'll tend the horses and stock same as before, and I'll have someone to keep an eye on me."

Pete Lorda hesitated, then decided against telling Tex what he could anticipate in the way he might act. "Get your shirt and hat and let's go."

Michel and Grant watched the pickup speed through the main gate to the highway that would take it to Carson.

"Will he die?" Michel asked Grant.

"I don't know," said Grant, and left Michel standing while he went to gather up the things he would need to stay with Ramon. Lorda had delegated him the task, and Grant had consented to go. When he emerged from the bunkhouse, he was carrying a thin bedroll and wearing a buckskin jacket with Indian fringes.

"You going to have to do all my work," he told Michel. "I'm going on vacation, loafing on my horse and shooting coyotes."

"I don't know how to shoe a horse," said Michel.

"You don't have to," Grant called back. "All the riding horses are shoed solid." He made his way to the gate that opened onto the horse pasture and whistled. His horse, a red-and-white mustang, came trotting to him. Grant saddled the mustang and tied on his bedroll with the leather thongs behind the saddle. Then he was off in a quick trot toward Ramon's band of year- lings. Tristant, the old sheepherder, came to stand with Michel as he watched Grant ride away.

"We got double work to do now," he said. "Things are getting worse instead of better."

The ax head came down and split the log cleanly in two. The woodpile for Mama Lorda's big stove and the bunkhouses was growing steadily. It was already big enough to satisfy the ranch's needs for the week to come.

Marie had been watching Michel from the kitchen window. His lean strong arms did not escape her attention. From time to time, she took a pitcher of lemonade out on the back stoop. "You got to rest sometime," she said to Michel.

"This cottonwood you have here on the ranch is easy to chop," said Michel. "In the Basque Country, it was my job to chop oak wood for the big fireplace where the cooking was done in our house. Oak is very hard to cut, but it burns a long time."

They sat together in the spring sun as Michel answered her questions about life in the Old Country. She was insatiable in her curiosity.

"Do you have a sweetheart back there?" she asked. Michel shook his head. "No. I have nothing to offer a girl. In a family of four boys, the youngest cannot look forward to much. In the Basque way, the property passes to the oldest son. The rest either go to seminary to become priests, or go to the village to apprentice themselves to an artisan—a shoemaker, carpenter, or whatever. The youngest son goes to the Americas, either North or South. If he goes to South America, he learns Spanish and becomes a gaucho. If he goes to North America, he learns English and becomes a sheepherder."

"Why did you choose the United States?"

"Because this is where the opportunity is, and the money," said Michel. "Anyway, your father asked my family if I would come to help him on his ranch. Naturally, they said yes. He paid for my passage on the boat, and I must repay him that out of my wages."

"Are you sorry?"

Michel shook his head emphatically. "No. This is paradise. I have my clothes and my boots and my necessities bought for me. I have a wool jacket for winter. The work is easy compared to the Basque Country. I am learning English better every day. And your father puts part of my wages in the bank to save for me. What more could I ask for?"

"When you have enough money, will you go home and find a girl to marry?"

Michel blushed. "No, I have nobody I want to go back for." He avoided her eyes and picked up his ax. "I must go back to work. Your father is not paying me to be lazy."

CHAPTER 14

Nazario the sheepherder gazed in bewilderment at the carnage that surrounded him. The torn bodies of lambs and ewes were scattered through the sagebrush around the carcasses of coyotes that had been shot by him and Slim.

Not even Lorda had anticipated this slaughter. Coyotes already rabid and mindless had come out of the hills to fasten and tear at every lamb or its mother. Even the roar of gunfire had failed to frighten them off. They had only one thing in their minds—to bite and kill the vulnerable prey they had killed through the years.

With rifles and pistols, Nazario and Slim had blunted the first wave of frothing coyotes that had come down upon them, but they were helpless to shoot the coyotes that had come under the concealment of night. It was only with the coming of daylight that they could see what they were aiming at. But so many! Doctor Cady had been right when he guessed that the desert hills were home to a hundred coyotes that had proliferated without interruption for God knows how long.

When Slim came riding back to replenish his store of cartridges for both pistol and rifle, his horse was lathered with sweat. It seemed to Nazario that he had been shooting steadily since daylight.

Sheep and lambs were still scattered over the desert. In the lull, Nazario prepared to set out with his sheepdog, Campolo, to round them up.

"If I wasn't seeing this with my own eyes," Slim said to Nazario, "I wouldn't believe it. Pity the poor rancher in times like this!"

When Pete Lorda finally made his appearance on horseback, he looked the part of a man who could use pity. Until he had mustered his reserve and demeanor, his face was blanched and his shoulders were slumped. He knew he was looking not only at the massacre of his carefully nurtured band of mothers and lambs, but at the loss of his earnings for the year. He was facing ruin, and he knew it. Only a miracle could save him if fate continued to go against him.

Lorda rode wordlessly through nature's ravage, pausing only to stare down at a ewe or a lamb he had praised earlier as superior.

After he had made his circuit, he came back to Nazario's camp. He took the cup of coffee laced with whiskey that Nazario handed him and sipped it gratefully.

"We got to go back to the ranch," he said sternly. "The bastards have beaten us on the open range. At least we can feed the flock until the hay runs out. With one hell of a lot of luck, we could make it without losing too many head from no feed."

"If you change your mind," said Slim, "I'm game to stay up here with Nazario."

"No. It's a losing game. Let's don't make it any worse than it is," said Lorda. "But I thank you anyway."

"They could make a living," Nazario said. "If the spring grass comes earlier."

"We'll damn soon find out," said Lorda.

CHAPTER 15

P ete Lorda had not gotten back from his horseback ride to Nazario's camp. Tristant was pitching hay to the saddle horses in their field. Tex was flat on his back in the bunkhouse, sick from the effects of the huge needle of serum the doctor had pumped into the lining of his stomach. Michel, coming back from feeding the bummer orphan lambs that had collected, had time on his hands before his next round of chores.

The border collie on the end of his chain was eyeing Michel. For once, his hackles were not raised, and this gave rise to Michel's curiosity. He stopped on his way into the bunkhouse to appraise the unexpectedly passive dog. Intrigued, he decided to have a closer look.

When he did, it was with an exclamation of surprise. The pot of milk was empty. The dog had drunk its contents.

"*Jesu!*" he exclaimed in Basque. "You got well like I said you would."

Still, Michel approached the dog warily. His close call with getting bitten the last time he had approached the dog was not forgotten. Michel inched forward on the balls of his feet until he was standing almost over the dog. He stood with every muscle tensed to jump away.

When nothing happened, Michel leaned over with his hands on his knees. Again, the dog neither moved away nor cowered.

Michel spoke to him in soft Basque tones. "I'm going to pet you now," he murmured. "Please, oh, please don't bite me."

Michel's hand moved downward until it was right above the dog's ears. Still, the dog did not get up. Only his eyes moved, following Michel's hand.

Michel lowered his hand until his fingertips could feel the tips of the dog's hair. He lowered his hand until it rested on the dog's head.

When the collie struck, there was absolutely no warning. The dog's canine teeth slashed across the palm of Michel's hand. It was not a gentle attack. The dog had bitten Michel so deeply that he yelped in pain. He backed away quickly and looked at the blood pouring out of the deep groove across his palm. Now, the dog's hackles were up and his lips were curled, ready to attack again.

Michel regarded his hand in horror. It was a bloody mess, but his instincts told him that the outpouring of blood was cleansing the wound, and with it, he prayed, forcing out the deadly virus he had been warned about. He ran to the pump and let its full force wash onto his hand until the wound stopped bleeding.

Michel was caught on the horns of a dilemma. He knew he should get help from a doctor immediately. But his stubborn insistence that he could cure his dog by himself suffused him with guilt. The contemplation of the scorn and anger that could descend on him made him mute and powerless to seek help. Pete Lorda might even send him back to the Basque Country. Yet something had to be done. Recalling what Tex had done to treat his wound, he went inside the bunkhouse and found the bottle of sheep-dip. Tex was still deep in sleep from the sedative the doctor had given him to withstand the painful side effects of the rabies serum.

Finding a clean ranch bandanna in his clothes sack, Michel went outside. The burning he expected did not deter him one bit. He unscrewed the cap on the bottle and poured the sheep-dip directly into the wound. The burning sensation drew a muffled groan from him, but he clenched his teeth and withstood it. When the pain had subsided, he soaked the bandanna in sheep-dip, wrapped it around his hand, and knotted it with the help of his teeth. When the operation was done, he went inside and found a new pair of leather gloves that Marie had given him, and pulled one over his hand to conceal the wound and the bandage.

Michel had determined not to tell anyone that he had been bitten by a rabid dog. He could not see how any germ or virus, as Doctor Cady called it, could survive the bleeding out and the burning sheep-dip.

As for the dog, the decision needed no second thought. Michel took one of the light rifles in the bunkhouse off its pegs, loaded it, and went outside to shoot the dog before it could bite either a person or one of the working sheepdogs. He buried his dog in the sagebrush without emotion. At the least, he had tried to save its life. Now, it was his own life to think about. He set his mind to come up with an excuse for his injured hand.

Michel had purposely delayed joining the procession to the dinner table. He did not want to attract anyone's attention to his bandaged hand. But he was not to be successful. Marie met him before he had a chance to join the others for dinner.

"Are you going to eat with a glove on?" she said teasingly.

Michel flushed and pulled off the glove that concealed the bandanna he had wrapped over the border collie's bite.

"You hurt your hand," said Marie. "That's a terrible-looking bandage."

"It's good enough," said Michel. "I just cut my hand a little, sharpening the ax."

"It's *not* good enough," Marie said. "You had better let me put a proper bandage on the cut."

Michel knew there was no arguing with Marie. She was as stubborn as he. "All right," he said reluctantly. "Can we wait until after dinner? There'll be nothing left if I don't hurry up. These are hungry men."

Marie shook her head decisively. "We doctor it now, before it can get infected. If it isn't infected already." She took him by the arm and led him to a table under the medicine cabinet. When the bandanna had been stripped off, she made a sound of mixed disgust and sympathy. "That's an ugly cut," she said. "It probably needs stitches."

"No doctor!" Michel said with an edge of anger in his voice. "It will heal up in a hurry."

Marie cleaned the wound and daubed the cut with iodine. Michel winced but made no sound to reveal his pain. Marie took his hand in her own and wrapped it with gauze and tape. It was the second time they had touched, and their feeling for each other revealed itself in their eyes.

"All right," said Marie. "You can have your dinner now. But I will need to dress your hand again tomorrow after work. Keep the dirt out of it. You were right in wearing a glove."

Pete Lorda's face was gray with the experience he had gone through at the band of ewes and lambs Nazario was herding. He was describing what had happened. "It was a massacre," he said, his voice trembling with anger. "Not counting the mothers, but all those beautiful lambs with their throats ripped out." He explained that he had ordered Nazario and Slim to drive the survivors of the band back to the ranch. The ewes would be fed on hay remaining in the stacks in the fields. "It's going to be a big job, but we got no choice. We got to keep them alive until the spring grass grows." He stopped and crossed himself. "Or the epidemic stops. God knows we've killed enough coyotes. And a lot more should have died of the rabies by now."

"What does the veterinarian say?" Michel asked.

"He says it's got to end pretty soon," said Lorda. "Meeker's men have killed at least a hundred coyotes. There can't be that many still alive."

"What happened to your hand?" Lorda said to Michel.

"I cut it sharpening the ax," Michel said, his voice evasive under Lorda's judging gaze. "Marie fixed it up."

"There will be one hell of a lot of pitching hay to Nazario's band," said Lorda. "Can you handle your part of the work?"

"It's nothing," said Michel. "It's just a scratch."

"That's a lot of bandage for a little scratch," said Lorda. "I've got to take Tex in for his serum shot tomorrow. Maybe you better come with me and let the doctor look at it."

Michel paled. "I don't need a doctor," he said insistently. "Don't worry. I'll do my part in pitching hay."

"Well . . ." Lorda said doubtfully, then decided to let the matter drop. "Keep an eye on it."

"Marie's going to do that," said Michel.

Lorda smiled for the first time. "That shouldn't be a pain for you."

"It won't be," said Michel. "She's a good doctor." He turned his attention to eating his dinner clumsily, with his left hand. He chose not to mention it, but the bite on his right hand was beginning to feel strange. It was a sensation Michel had never experienced before through all the cuts his hands had suffered both at his home farm in the Basque Country and here doing his duties at Pete Lorda's ranch.

CHAPTER 16

On the third day after the border collie had bitten him, Michel woke up with a headache and a sore throat.

It was no ordinary headache. His temples were pounding so painfully that he had to press his hands to the sides of his head in an effort to ease the throbbing.

From across the bunkhouse, the old shepherd Tristant was sitting on his bunk, tying his boots. He raised his eyes to regard Michel. "You got yourself a bad headache, ain't you? It couldn't have come from the wine at dinner. You only had two cups."

"No, I didn't get drunk," Michel croaked. He felt his throat. "I got a sore throat, too. I must've of caught a cold."

"Take a couple aspirin with your coffee at breakfast," said Tristant. "Marie's got plenty in her medicine cabinet." Tristant put on his flannel-lined Levi's jacket against the morning chill and went out the door.

At the end of the bunkhouse, Tex was pulling on his boots. His face had a sickly pallor to it. "Another day, another shot," he groaned. "Sometimes I think the cure is worse than the rabies. I can't keep anything down."

Instead of being the first man out the door on his way to breakfast, Michel was the last. When he was dressed, he went to the wash bench and listlessly scrubbed his face and hands with soap and water.

He was the last in line as the ranch crew trooped into Mama Lorda's kitchen. He had no appetite, but he knew he had to go through the pretense of eating. On his way to the table, he said hello to Mama Lorda and nodded a greeting to Marie. She was eyeing him questioningly.

"It's time to change your bandage," she said to Michel. "We'll do it right after breakfast." She paused, and then added in a whisper, "You don't look well. In fact, you look sick."

"I'm all right," said Michel unconvincingly. "Maybe I got a cold coming on. Tristant says I better ask you for some aspirin."

"He's probably right," said Marie. "How do you feel sick?" She reached out and pressed her palm on Michel's forehead. "You got a little fever," she said. "What else?"

"Headache," said Michel.

"And a sore throat," said Marie. "Your voice is hoarse."

"I'm sorry," said Michel.

"Don't apologize," said Marie. "Everybody gets sick sometime. Come see me after breakfast. I'll have some aspirin ready."

Pete Lorda looked back over his shoulder to see what was happening. Knowing that Michel would not confess to a weakness, Marie told her father, "Michel's sick."

"How sick?" Lorda said in exasperation. "Too sick to work? When Nazario's band shows up, things are going to be awfully busy around here. We'll be pitching hay until our arms drop off."

"I'm not too sick to work," Michel said with an irritation he had not displayed before.

"Good," said Lorda. "You can start spreading hay this morning. It can be waiting for Nazario's band when it shows up this afternoon. Spread it thin. That's not much hay for that many ewes."

When breakfast was done, Michel dutifully took his cleared plate to Mama Lorda's sink and dropped it into the soapy water. Marie summoned him to her medicine cabinet, making him take two aspirin before she began dressing his hand.

"That cut's not healing the way it should," she said. "It's festering even with the iodine on it. I think you better see a doctor. You can go along when Tex goes in for his shot."

"No," said Michel angrily. "I'm not going to a doctor."

Marie was startled. Michel had never displayed a temper before. He was shy and polite to a fault, so much so that Marie had been tempted to lecture him about the dangers of subservience to the other men on the ranch crew.

"All right," she said. "It's your life. I'm just trying to help."

At her mention of his "life," Michel recoiled and regarded her searchingly. He wondered if he was gambling with death if he was infected with rabies, then dismissed the fear. "I'll be all right by tomorrow. Watch and see."

CHAPTER 17

B ut Michel was *not* all right by the next day. He worked steadily all the day through, but it was an effort of will. At day's end, he threw himself on his bunk in exhaustion.

Tristant was regarding him soberly. He was puzzled by Michel's weariness. He had always been a tireless worker. "What happened to your dog?" he asked with sudden suspicion. "Did he bite you? Is that what's the matter with your hand?"

"No, no, no," said Michel, bridling. "He came close is all. There was no curing him, I found out."

Tristant was silent. He knew something had happened, and he had a good idea what it had been. "If you say so," he muttered.

When the dinner bell sounded, Tristant got to his feet. "We better wash up," he said. "You better not get Mama Lorda mad at you."

Michel did not stir from his bunk. "You go ahead," he said. "I'm not hungry."

Tristant crossed the bunk room to stand over Michel. "After all the work we did today, you got to be hungry."

"Well, I'm not," Michel said angrily. "I've got no appetite."

"Then you must be sick," said Tristant. He leaned over Michel. "Your face is red. Have you got a fever?"

"That's none of your business," said Michel. "Go to dinner and leave me alone."

But Tristant was adamant. "Mama Lorda is going to ask me where you are. What am I supposed to tell her?"

"Tell her I got a cold," said Michel. "Tell her anything. Just leave me alone."

Tristant was concerned, not about Michel's refusal to go to dinner, but about his flare of anger. In the months Michel had been with the Lorda ranch, he had never uttered an angry word.

"Did you get aspirin from Marie?" he asked with worry in his voice. When Michel cried yes, Tristant said, "I'll ask Marie for some more. You sure as hell need something, if not for your cold, then your temper."

Michel leaped off his bunk and thrust his face forward. "Will you leave me alone?" he shouted.

Tristant backed away. "All right, all right," he said. "You don't have to yell at me." He turned and shambled out the bunkhouse door. As he washed himself at the pump, he said to himself, *Something is sure as hell wrong with that boy.*

N azario's band of ewes and lambs began trailing into the ranch pastures in the early morning. Their feed was ready for them, scattered in clumps across the first blush of spring green. The ewes were hungry and moved at a trot toward the clumps of rich alfalfa hay.

After they had satisfied their first hunger, a number of the ewes milled with the band, bleating hopelessly for their lambs that had been slaughtered by the horde of rabid coyotes.

Pete Lorda, pitchfork in hand, moved grimly across the pasture, scattering the clumps of hay even more. The day before, Lorda, Tristant, and Michel had thrown up temporary wire fences around the haystacks to protect them from being overrun with sheep. Tristant and Michel were leading in an immense hay wagon with hay that would be scattered across the pasture for the next feeding.

Michel was making a point of avoiding Lorda while he worked. At breakfast, Michel had waved aside the questions about his missing dinner. He forced himself to go through the motions of eating his ham and eggs and hotcakes, but he had been unsuccessful in swallowing any coffee. His throat was constricted, refusing any liquid.

Despite his exhaustion, Michel had spent a sleepless night tossing on his bunk. As much as his body cried for slumber, he could not sleep. His face was drawn with fatigue.

"You look terrible," Marie had whispered to him when he passed through the breakfast line.

"It will pass," Michel answered hoarsely. "Just give it time." Nevertheless, he did not refuse the aspirin Marie handed to him.

"I'm going to tell my father you're a sick man," she said.

"Don't," Michel pleaded with her. "Not today of all times. You can't believe how much work we've got waiting for us."

"I'll wait one more day," said Marie. "If you're not any better by tomorrow, I promise you you're going to see the doctor."

The urge to run began to torment Michel on the fifth day after he had been bitten. It was as if the muscles of his legs were on fire with the need to run as far and fast as he could. His body was tired beyond measure with the ceaseless pitching of hay to hungry ewes, yet it still needed to run itself to further exhaustion.

The ranch crew was well on its way to demolishing one mountainous stack of hay, but this was not enough to satisfy the sheep. They had even begun to paw at the meager spring grass that was beginning to grow in the confines of the pasture.

Pete Lorda was tempted to turn the entire band loose in the sagebrush that surrounded the ranch, but he could not risk another slaughter from the coyotes that he felt were waiting in the desert hills.

Sick as he was, Tex was still circling the pasture with rifle in hand and pistol at the ready. Twice, their nights had been interrupted by the drumming of sheep hooves in panic, and twice Tex had ridden out with a flashlight to find an invading coyote. That had been enough to make up Lorda's mind to keep the band of ewes in the pasture. The only consolation he had was that the incidents could have been worse. A dozen coyotes at a time could have leapt the fences to wreak havoc with the ewes and their fragile lambs.

When suppertime came, Marie was there to examine Michel's appearance to see if he was getting better.

Pete Lorda did not help Michel's cause a bit. When the crew sat down at the table, he said to Michel, "You're as thin as a pole. What's the matter with you?"

That decided Marie. When dinner was done and she was dressing Michel's hand, she told him emphatically, "You're going to the doctor tomorrow whether you like it or not. This has gone far enough."

"You'll make me lose my job. We're shorthanded as it is for all the hay that needs to be scattered." It was his final argument. He knew when the running urge had come over him that something was desperately wrong with his health. He nodded his head and consented to Marie's demands.

CHAPTER 19

Michel's body was crying for sleep, but his quivering nerves would not let him even close his eyes. Under the flannel blankets, his body was strung as tight as a violin string. On ordinary nights, Tristant's snoring had not bothered him, but tonight it was infuriating. It told him that the old sheepherder was deep in the kind of restful slumber that Michel craved.

Michel opened his eyes and stared through the high window that served to light the bunkhouse in the daytime. The moon was out and filled the window with its lurid pallor. Michel stared at it as though he were hypnotized by the shadows of clouds moving across its surface. In an indefinable way, the moon seemed to be calling to him. Since sleep was impossible, he decided to go outside to observe it more closely.

He dressed as quietly as he could, so as not to wake Slim in his bunk at the end of the bunkhouse. His work boots scraping on the wooden floor betrayed him as he got to the door. Slim cleared his throat and said, "Where you going, kid?"

"I can't sleep," Michel said. "I'm going for a walk."

"Good God," said Slim. "After all the work we did today, you should sleep like a rock. Ain't you tired?"

"No, I'm not tired," Michel lied. "I need to walk."

"Well, more power to you," said Slim. "You're going to be dragging ass tomorrow."

Michel said nothing. He stepped through the door into the night outside. The moon lighted the corrals and the sleeping sheep. A lamb mewed for its mother, and the mother answered. In the far pasture, a horse nickered. From the direction of the ranch house, a dog barked to signal that it had heard him. Michel found the lane that led beyond the corrals to the desert and lengthened his stride. The extra effort seemed to calm his nerves, and he kept on walking.

Michel had no destination in mind. All that lay in front of him were the desert hills that led to the high peaks, but not the peaks that were grazing land. As the terrain grew steeper, his legs began to tire, but he welcomed the fatigue as though it were medicine.

After an hour, his body told him that he should stop and rest, but his legs would not let him stop. They propelled him forward in spite of himself. When finally his legs buckled under him, he knew that something was going wrong in his mind.

He realized he was doing a foolish thing, but he was captive to movement. He had fallen on his face with no feeling. Then fright came to him, and he rolled over onto his knees, looked at the sky, and in his helplessness began to pray.

But there was no answer to be found in his pleas to the heavens. The sky looked down on him without compassion. Michel closed his eyes and tried to remember his home. He saw his mother and father sitting on their bench beside the great fireplace where the family spent their time until sleep overtook them and they trailed off to bed. He tried to remember making his way to the room where he slept and the shelter of his feather bed that had always given him protection in the times of childhood fears. He longed desperately for home.

His imagining and need gave him surcease from the compulsion that was driving him, but it was not to be for long. Against his will, he struggled to his feet and resumed climbing the rocky slope, fighting his way through the sagebrush and clambering over the boulders that blocked his way. By the time he reached the top of the first hill, his clothes were in shreds, and what was worse, his hands were beginning to bleed.

When the moon had waned and the first pale hue of dawn began to lighten the sky, Michel was still climbing. By then, he had lost all feeling and most of his senses. Twice, he had narrowly averted walking over the edge of an abandoned mine shaft east of the ranch. It was unfamiliar ground. He had ventured into mining country, and the shaft had led to silver ore sixty years earlier. When the silver was exhausted, the miners had simply walked away, leaving the scars of their digging unhealed.

When daylight bathed the valley, Michel had climbed high enough into the rising peaks that he could not see the ranch or the pastures that lay beyond them. The realization brought naked fear to what was left of his senses. He had lost direction and did not know where his trembling legs would finally take him. He collapsed again, and this time he fainted. Unconsciousness flooded over him.

CHAPTER 20

W hat do you mean, 'he went for a walk,'" Pete Lorda said angrily. "In the middle of the night?"

"I'm telling you like it happened," said Slim defensively.

"Where did he go?"

"How in hell do I know?" said Slim. "I thought I would see him here for breakfast."

"Did any of the rest of you see him go or where he went?" Lorda asked the men of the crew gathered for breakfast in Mama Lorda's kitchen.

But no one had seen Michel anywhere on the ranch or in the fields outside of it. "Well, eat your breakfast, and then we'll search the barns and the pens. I thought he had more sense than this business of going for a walk."

Marie had come from helping her mother at the stove. "I don't like the sound of this, Papa. Michel hasn't been himself for days now. He must be sick."

"In the head, yes," said Lorda with an edge in his voice. "To do a foolish thing like this."

"I didn't mean it that way," said Marie. "I mean seriously sick. Like the rabies. That cut on his hand. Michel says he cut his hand chopping wood. But it's not getting well like it should. I know. I've been treating him."

"Good God!" Lorda exclaimed. "If he's got the rabies, we better find him in a hurry. What did Doctor Cady say? The rabies can kill a man in a week unless he's treated." He gulped down the rest of his coffee. "If he's taken off into the hills, we'll play hell finding him."

"The Indian can track him," said Tex.

"But Grant is with Ramon's band," said Lorda. "We've got to get him back here. Tex, are you up to riding to Ramon's camp?"

"I'm weak," said Tex. "But not so weak I can't ride to Ramon's camp."

Marie caught at Lorda's sleeve as he was going out the door. "Find him, Papa," she said. "He's a good young man."

Pete Lorda was surprised to see tears clouding Marie's eyes. He took her hand. "Don't worry. Grant can track a lizard. He'll find Michel."

Grant walked nearly doubled over as he scrutinized the ground. Pete Lorda, riding his own horse and leading Grant's pinto, followed behind.

It had been slow going from the bunkhouse to the lane that led between the corrals. Grant had learned to identify the track outside the bunkhouse, but Michel's tracks had been mingled with men and sheep tracks until the main lane through the corrals had ended and the open desert began. The going was easier then, but the track wove tortuously through the sagebrush and the granite rock formations on a route different from the one the ranch used.

"The kid's headed to mining country," Grant said to Lorda.

"I don't like that. It's loose ground up there, and it's covered with mine shafts from the old days. They're hard to see in the dark. He could fall in."

Pete Lorda was perplexed. "What in God's name would draw him up there?"

Grant tapped his temple. "He's wrong in the head is all I can think. His track doesn't go anywhere but up. But what the hell's up there?"

As the day wore on, Pete Lorda was becoming more concerned. He chastised himself for not insisting that Michel see the doctor in town when he had been bitten by the border collie. But the young man was stubborn and would not hear of it. If the bite had given him the rabies, he would probably die unless they could get him on the serum that Tex had been subjected to. But they had to find him first. Lorda's memory jogged back to Marie's tears, and he became doubly worried. Tears could mean that she had fallen in love with Michel.

To add to his worries, Grant said, "Daylight is going fast. We can't track him at night. If we don't find him before dark, we got to go back to the ranch and come here in the morning." He was silent. "What bothers me is that he hasn't stopped to rest, not even once. That don't make sense to me. This is steep country. Any man would have stopped to rest by now. Not once, but a good five times. My own legs are ready to fold."

They went on until dusk made it impossible to go farther, then marked the place well for the next day's tracking.

"You know something else?" Grant asked Lorda.

"What?"

"We haven't seen a coyote all day. What does that mean?"

"You're right," said Lorda. "If it means what I hope it does, I'll be a happy man. Maybe the worst is over."

A grim and doleful greeting met Lorda and Grant when they rode into the ranch without Michel. Lorda anticipated their questions as he swung down from his saddle at dusk in front of the ranch house. "No, we didn't find him, but Grant has cut his track. We followed it until the light gave out on us."

"Thank God you didn't find him dead," said Marie with a catch in her voice.

Pete Lorda took her in his arms. "We might before it's over, but I just don't think so. He's probably walked himself out and is lying in some sagebrush to keep warm."

"*Gauchua*. Poor thing," Mama Lorda said in Basque.

"*Ergela*. Foolish thing would be closer to the truth. Thinking he could cure that dog with milk."

"I want to ride up the mountain with you," said Marie. "I want to be there when you find him."

Pete Lorda shook his head. "No, you're not coming with us. In case the worst has happened, it won't be a pretty sight."

The cowboys Slim and Tex joined in. "We could fan out and help search for him. Four of us can cover a lot of country."

"There's plenty of work to do here," said Lorda, "scattering hay. Those ewes are looking gaunt already. If their milk dries up without feed, we'll have a mess of starved lambs on our hands."

"Funny thing," said Grant. "We didn't see a coyote all day. Did any come down here to tear up ewes or lambs?"

"Slim and I were thinking the same thing," said Tex. "We didn't have any trouble at all."

"Let me call the doc," said Lorda. "He can tell us if the worst is over."

"Please God," said Mama Lorda. "Let it be so."

Pete Lorda dropped his reins. "Groom them good," said Lorda to Tristant. "I want Grant with me when I telephone the doctor. He can answer questions you can't."

"Yes," said Grant. "I want to find out why Michel is walking so crazy. He don't act like he knows where he's going."

Pete Lorda's voice was cautiously optimistic as he talked on the telephone to the veterinarian. "Am I hearing you right? Is the worst of it over?"

There was a long pause as Lorda listened to what Doctor Cady was telling him. Then he said, "I know you can't be sure, but if anyone can make a good guess, it's you. You say Meeker tells you the same thing I'm telling you. That has to be good news. How about the other sheep ranchers?"

There was another pause, and then Lorda said, "That means there's still some sick coyotes out there, but a hell of a lot less than we've been seeing. Right? Right."

Pete Lorda's tone became personal and worried. "You know young Michel, the ranch hand with the border collie he was trying to cure? Let me tell you what's happened to him. I want your advice." Lorda described what was happening and the fruitless day of tracking that Grant and he had had. "We had to quit when night came on," Lorda concluded. "But we're going out to pick up the track at daylight." Lorda's responses to Doctor Cady's questions were almost confined to yes and no. When he was done, he hung up the telephone and turned to the group that was gathered around him.

"We guessed right," he said. "The worst part of the rabies epidemic looks like it's almost over. With the coyotes we and the other ranchers have been shooting and the ones that have died from the disease, there don't seem to be many alive out there. And the rabies could be moving, to another part of the range, or even California. It don't stay in one place, the doc says."

Sighs and exclamations of relief came from the group, except for Marie.

"What did he say about Michel running away?"

Pete Lorda's tone became grave. "The way Michel has been acting—the short temper, the taking off at night, and worst of all, the cut on his hand—all points to one thing: rabies. The doc can't be sure, but it doesn't look good." He paused and then asked without warning, "Did Michel take a gun with him?"

"What are you saying? He might shoot somebody?"

"Or himself," said Tristant, the old herder.

"Or anyone coming after him," said Grant. "Like the boss or me."

Slim tried to calm their fears. "He wasn't carrying a rifle that I could see when he left the bunkhouse."

"Papa," said Marie with a constricted voice, "could he have gone crazy? Why do you ask that?"

Pete Lorda reached out and took Marie in his arms. "Because if he does have the rabies, he'll be out of his head."

CHAPTER 21

Michel woke in the first light, wondering where he was and how he had gotten there. He had wandered into a grove of piñon pines, and when night came on, he had been dreadfully cold. Out of instinct, he had dug himself a hole in a mound of piñon needles for warmth. He was still shaking from the cold, but at least the covering of pine needles had kept him from freezing. In the pale light of dawn, the trees towering above him were ghostly pinnacles, but the first rays of the sun had already touched their tips. Michel watched the sun's rays as they ascended. Sun would mean warmth, but he was reluctant to leave his bed of pine needles until the sun reached him.

He did not know it, but he was in one of the respites that accompanies the disease that had claimed him. He could remember practically nothing of the day before and the night that followed it. There were vague images in which the faces of people and their voices appeared and then disappeared. He was dreadfully tired and ravenously thirsty. When he touched his face tentatively, it was like touching dried leather. His lips were cracked, and when he opened his mouth, he felt his lips crack even further, and he tasted blood.

When finally he thought about people, a flare of anger seared his brain. Where were they and how could they have left him in the condition he was in? That reaction was set off by the sight of his arm when he lifted it. The jacket and the shirt that had covered it were in shreds, and the skin underneath was torn and bleeding. How could this be when he could not remember what had brought about this situation?

The sound of running water came to him, and his dehydrated body told him he must go to it before anything else. He sat up and looked around, and saw that he was lying near a creek of running water. He crawled to it and plunged his face into the water and drank great gulps of the life-giving fluid. Being able to drink made him remember that before, his throat would not permit him to swallow, and he wondered why that had been. The effort to remember set off a chain of painful memories—the absolute fatigue that his legs had known, the refusal of his body to stop for rest, the tearing of his flesh as he clambered through barbed bitterbrush and over the unyielding rock formations, and finally, the black veil of unconsciousness that had fallen over him and the jarring impact of his falling to the ground.

He was afraid to take the next step of mind to where it had all begun, but he was helpless to stop the flow of memory. He raised his hand, and the bloody gash across the palm told him all. The knowledge that he had contracted rabies that would kill him horribly flooded over him, and tears coursed down through the dirt on his face.

He groped for surcease in the knowledge that he was normal now, and then the realization came to him that it was only temporary, that the torture would return. His legs jerked, and he knew it was beginning. But he also knew that he would not permit himself to go on living in that tortured state. He had denied it to himself before he lost consciousness, but he would not choose to undergo it again. Somehow, he must kill himself. And then he remembered the mine shafts he had narrowly averted falling into and knew that was the answer he sought. He was helpless to stop his legs from raising his body to a standing position, but at least he knew what he was looking for.

Even before first light, Pete Lorda and Grant were well on their way to where they had given up tracking Michel because of falling darkness. Grant with his Indian instincts had led the way, and Lorda followed, leading an extra horse to carry Michel home, dead or alive.

Marveling at the sure pace of Grant's weaving through the bitterbrush and rock formations in darkness, Pete Lorda held out hope that they would find Michel alive. How he would survive the night was another problem, but Michel's youth and physical toughness might make the difference. What they would find if the rabies had taken hold was something Lorda did not want to think about. His heart went out to his daughter. That Marie had fallen in love with Michel was undeniable. Lorda, who was not a religious man, crossed himself and breathed a silent prayer.

The morning sun had tipped the mountain rim when Lorda and Grant reached the place where Grant had given up trying to follow Michel's tracks. Grant swung down from his saddle to have a closer look at the tracks. "Good God," he exclaimed. "Get down and look at this one track."

Pete Lorda dismounted and bent over to see what Grant had found. The outline of Michel's boots were clear, but there was blood where the soles of his feet had touched earth. Pete Lorda gave a moan of pain. "He's bleeding, and he's still walking. He must be in terrible pain."

"And crazy as hell to keep on going," Grant said and bent over to follow Michel's trail. A shallow rock barrier loomed in front of them, and the tracks went up the face. Only now, there was added blood from torn hands and knees.

"He can't last much longer," said Grant. "He's losing more blood all the time. Crazy or not, his body is just plain giving out on him."

When they reached the rocky mountain rim, the horses began to lose their footing. Lorda and Grant tied their three horses head to tail, then led them lunging to the rim and better footing.

Michel's trail was easier to follow now. It led erratically but in one direction toward a grove of piñon pines with a creek running through it. When they entered the grove, they saw the depression and the scattered pine needles with which Michel had covered himself. "He must be getting his senses back," said Grant. "At least he tried to keep warm in the night."

Pete Lorda hitched his lead horse to a tree while they followed Michel's crawling passage on hands and knees to the creek. "He must be getting well," said Lorda. "He drank water, and that's one of the things the rabies won't let its victims do."

Grant shook his head doubtfully. "Don't count your horses until we find him. The doc said the spells come and go. He probably got his mind back, but I bet it's just for a little while. He didn't turn back to find the ranch and people who would help him. Something else is on his mind," he added seriously. "See where the tracks are leading. They're not going back to the ranch."

"I think you're right," said Lorda. "Let's get moving." They mounted, and Grant took up the track again.

It was Grant with his far-seeing Indian eyes who saw Michel's figure in the distance. The young man was staggering, but his movement showed he had a destination in mind. Grant pointed him out to Lorda, and they both shouted Michel's name. The young Basque turned briefly and saw them, but instead of coming to them, he continued his flight.

"What in hell's the matter with him?" Lorda cried.

Grant pointed at a derrick that marked the presence of a mine shaft. "That's what the matter with him is. He's going to throw himself into that shaft!"

Grant dug his spurs into his pinto's side, and the pinto leaped out in Michel's direction. As he rode, Grant shook out a loop from the lariat on his saddle. Lorda needed no further explanation. He spurred his horse after Grant, swearing because he had not brought along a lariat.

Michel was not to be deterred. He fell once, then got to his feet and made his way toward the mine shaft. He reached it and paused to look down into the black depths. Then, making up his mind, he was about to jump off the edge of the shaft when Grant's lariat circled his frame and brought him to an abrupt halt. Grant spurred his horse backward, dragging Michel out of the hole and onto level ground. But the boy was not giving up. Even though he was being pulled backward, his legs were scrambling in a forward movement.

Lorda pulled his horse to a stop and swung down from his saddle. He threw his hands around Michel's body and wrestled him to the ground. Michel's face was contorted, and he was screaming in protest. Working together, Lorda and Grant tied Michel's legs together and dragged him away from the mine shaft.

"Have you lost your mind?" Lorda shouted at him in Basque.

"No, I've found it," Michel gasped. "I don't want to die like a sick coyote."

Lorda held Michel until his struggles had eased and he started to cry. Lorda held him gently, but firmly, saying over and over, "You don't have to die! You will get well!"

He added gruffly, "If the rabies didn't kill you, Marie would have!"

CHAPTER 22

Michel was sitting on the edge of a hospital bed, his bandaged feet hanging over the side. They were still swathed in gauze and tape.

"Yes, you had the rabies," the doctor said. "But what's important is that you survived the disease. You didn't die, and you could have died horribly, the way things were going for you. You have to realize that you are one of the few people who have managed to live through it."

"Is it gone for good?" said Michel, his voice tremulous. "I don't want to go through that again. I dream of having to walk when my mind says no, but my body won't let me stop."

"You're not out of the woods yet," the doctor said. "But it's looking better all the time. You've had twenty shots now, and that's supposed to be enough to kill the rabies virus for good."

"Can I go back to the ranch?" Michel asked. "Marie tells me they've got a bedroom all ready."

"I think it will be all right for you to go home," the doctor said. "But if the symptoms flare up—fever and temperature, lack of orientation, being unable to swallow, not knowing where you are—you will have to come here for another series of shots. You do understand that?"

"How about my feet?" said Michel.

"They will take a while to heal," said the doctor. "You were down to bone. All that flesh you lost has to grow back. Marie has my instructions on how to care for them, which should be a pleasure for you. She's a pretty girl."

Michel blushed. "I know that. So I'm in no hurry to get healed."

And so the crisis passed, not only for Michel but for Pete Lorda and the sheep ranchers whose flocks had been ravaged by the disease that had appeared out of nowhere. No one knew where it came from, but it was done with now. The desert hills were littered with the bones of coyotes, bobcats, wildcats, mountain lions, and even skunks. Many of them had been shot to death, but the greatest killer had been the disease itself. Like the scourges of Europe, the rabies had run its course, and normalcy had returned to the land.